THE AUTHOR: Junnosuke Yoshiyuki was born in Okayama City in 1924. Drafted in 1943, he was sent home after three days with bronchial asthma. Two years later he entered Tokyo University, majoring in English literature, and in 1949 he published his first novel, *Bara Hambainin*. Another novel, *Genshoku no Machi*, was nominated for the Akutagawa Prize in 1952. In the same year, he was hospitalized with pulmonary tuberculosis, and two years later his left lung was removed. Among other novels published between 1954 and 1967 were *Shu-u* (Akutagawa Prize) and *Hoshi to Tsuki wa Ten no Ana* (Grand Prix, Minister of Education Awards). *The Dark Room* (*Anshitsu*), his first novel to be translated into English, appeared in 1970 and received the prestigious Tanizaki Prize. An earlier translation he made of four stories from Henry Miller's *Nights of Love and Laughter* was recently complemented by his Japanese version of Miller's *Insomnia or the Devil at Large*.

The Dark Room

JUNNOSUKE YOSHIYUKI

Translated by   JOHN BESTER

KODANSHA INTERNATIONAL LTD.

Tokyo, New York & San Francisco

First published in 1970 by Kodansha Ltd., Tokyo, as *Anshitsu*

Published by Kodansha International Ltd., 2-12-21 Otowa, Bunkyo-ku, Tokyo 112 and Kodansha International/USA Ltd., 10 East 53rd Street, New York 10022 and 44 Montgomery Street, San Francisco, California 94104. Copyright © 1975 by Kodansha International Ltd. All rights reserved. Printed in Japan.

LCC 75-11390
ISBN 0-87011-361-5
JBC 1093-786894-2361

First edition, 1975
Second paperback edition, 1978

1

She'd had it once, long ago—the grated bulb of some plant, wrapped in toasted seaweed and deep-fried in oil—and enjoyed it. She'd thought to try it again, and was still thinking, fifty years later. . . .

The essay, by a woman novelist, had stuck in my memory. Strange, I thought, how you can have something on your mind to do, but before you do it, fifty long years have slipped by. And yet, I thought again, how often it happens. . . .

I have a mole under my right eye. "Weeping moles," they're called, or so they told me when I was a kid. Not a very lucky thing to have, I reflected at the time, and gave the matter no further thought.

"Weeping mole"—the phrase seems to mean something, but when you think about it you're not at all sure what. I must have been around twenty when that first occurred to me. A book on physiognomy, I reflected, would certainly have something more definite to say on the subject. I'd no particular faith in such works, but at least if I looked it up it would replace uncertainty with a definite shape of some kind. But though I meant to do so, I was still meaning to do so twenty years later.

The essay about the vegetable reminded me of it. I remembered having some myself at a tempura restaurant, and reflected rather impatiently that you could, after all, make the dish at home if you wanted to. But then, I still hadn't done anything about my mole, had I?

A few months later, I was at a meeting when an acquaintance of mine who sports a beard came up and without warning ran a finger round the edge of my ear.

"I can tell you're not an eldest son."

"But I am."

"That's odd. The shape of your ear says you aren't. Did you have an elder brother who died, then?"

"No, I've no elder brothers or sisters."

"Well then, perhaps they got rid of a kid before you were born?"

"I don't think so. That kind of thing wasn't so easy, you know, in those days."

He looked disgruntled.

"Studying physiognomy?" I asked.

"That's right."

"Tell me then—what does this mole of mine mean?"

It didn't matter whether the answer was scientific or not. What I wanted, you see, was some definite reply. The bearded friend contemplated my face.

"Mm, under the right eye. . . . That's an easy one: your girl will give you trouble."

" 'Girl'? You mean my daughter?"

"That's right."

I was taken aback. I'd been quite sure it would be something about myself.

"My daughter, eh? When you say 'trouble'? . . ."

"Well, like having bad health, or getting mixed up with the wrong kind of man."

"I see. . . ."

"Ah, I've got you interested this time! I didn't know you had a daughter, though."

"I don't," I said. "No kids at all."

2

A few days later, I was by myself in a bar leading off the lobby of a small hotel. Seated on my tall stool, I looked at the clock on the wall. A little after 10 P.M.

They were broadcasting canned music in the lobby and bar that night. It was a few days before Christmas, and the tune was of the kind they make you so sick of around the same time every year. Sipping my whisky, I absentmindedly let the music wash over me.

Suddenly I noticed something. Another, different sound beneath the incessant flow of the music. A faint voice, like a woman sobbing. The woman's voice, thin and clear at first, thickened as the sobbing grew louder till finally it began to crack and heavy breathing mingled with it. The voice was already a fairly loud undercurrent beneath the music before I realized that it wasn't crying in distress.

The cries, I was quite certain, were cries of sexual ecstasy. Could some arrangement of ventilators and pipes be carrying noises or the sound of a tape recorder from one of the hotel rooms into the lobby?

I took a look around me. The four or five other men drinking at the bar all sat there with stolid expressions. I couldn't tell whether they were feigning indifference or just hadn't noticed. I gazed at the lobby through the glass that separated it from the bar, but no one sitting there seemed disturbed.

The man on the other side of the bar, an acquaintance with whom I exchanged the occasional off-color joke, was as expressionless as the rest. After a while he sensed my gaze on him and looked in my direction.

"The same again, sir?"

The woman's voice, though much quieter, was audible as ever. Suspecting my ears were playing me false, I listened again more carefully, but I could still hear it. Puzzled and disturbed at the same time, I remembered a similar feeling I'd had once before.

It came back to me without any effort.

I was at primary school, and an uncle had taken me to the movies. A cartoon was showing at the time. The one thing I remember clearly is that it was in technicolor, and the whole screen was occupied by a man's foot. The scene of the foot came again and again. All of a sudden, I noticed that the foot had six toes. I recounted them every time the foot appeared, but there were always six.

I looked at my uncle, who was sitting next to me. It was too dark to see his expression properly, but he seemed not to have noticed anything. I checked the other people about us, but the only reaction they showed was an occasional laugh.

"Say, Uncle . . ." I began in a small voice, nudging his arm with my elbow. With his eyes still on the screen, he took a box of caramels out of his pocket and handed it to me. My question deflected, I fell silent.

The cartoon was followed by a comedy, and when it was over we left.

"His foot had six toes, didn't it?" I ventured. Uncle looked at me doubtfully. "In the cartoon—," I explained, "there was a close-up of a foot, wasn't there?"

"Oh, ah. So there was."

"It had six toes!"

"Come off it!"

Uncle laughed and gave me a look of complete disbelief. I didn't feel like going back to the cinema to make sure, and even if I'd suggested it, Uncle would almost certainly not have agreed. . . .

When I awoke from my reminiscences, the Christmas music was still audible, but the other undercurrent of sound had ceased.

I recalled the voice in distress, feeling sure that it hadn't just been my imagination. As I did so, the faces of many women rose up in front of my eyes. These, beyond all doubt, *were* in my mind. Among them I could see the face of one who'd had an abortion because of me.

8

I remembered the conversation with my bearded friend a few days earlier. As we finished talking, I'd wondered to myself whether the baby we got rid of would have been a girl or a boy. Which of these women, then, had been the woman concerned?

I didn't hesitate. I turned straight to one of the faces lined up in the space before my eyes.

She was dead now, but she and I had once lived together as man and wife.

I'm forever getting dragged back into the past these days.

3

"Well, well—it's been a long time. How long exactly—ten years?"

The man's voice, sounding instant friendship in the depths of the receiver, was obviously familiar, but I couldn't place it.

"Who's calling, please?" I inquired in a formal voice.

"It's me, Tsunoki."

Toru Tsunoki: the tone had been so friendly I hadn't recognized him. But come to think of it, he'd spoken in just the same tone of voice when I'd met him ten years before.

"Oh, it's you, is it? This is quite an event."

At this point, I checked myself from saying, "And what are you doing these days?" My relationship with Tsunoki was a tricky business. His recent activities, I reflected, were probably one of the things I shouldn't inquire about.

Tsunoki, though, had no such misgivings.

"I hear you're lying pretty low these days. Seems you don't even get around town much."

"You seem to know a lot."

"It's not good for you, you know. You mustn't let yourself get negative about life."

I almost laughed out loud. Sensible advice, from someone like Tsunoki!

"You think 'life' is to be found around town?"

"Well, if you put it like *that* . . ." he said, a note of rueful amusement in his voice.

"The thing is," he went on, "I know a rather interesting bar—in fact I'm having a drink there now. Why don't you join me?"

"Interesting in exactly what way?"

I felt I couldn't be bothered. Incipient refusal must have crept into my voice, for Tsunoki turned abruptly high-handed.

"Come on, pull yourself out of that rut! After all, it's been ten years."

I said nothing.

"Actually," he went on, "it's much more. Ten years ago, we just exchanged a word or two in the street."

Suddenly, I felt an urge to take a closer look at this relationship that needed such careful handling. I agreed to join him.

Most of the space was taken up by the bar, with a single table you could sit round in one corner. Tsunoki was seated at the bar with a young man in tow.

With a brief nod, I sat down next to him. Three rather effeminate young men in white stood on the other side of the bar.

"The bartenders here are kind of, well, *womanly*, you know," Tsunoki whispered in my ear.

What a letdown, I thought: is *that* what Tsunoki finds so interesting about the place? I was silent, aware of his gaze on my profile. Before long he said in an oddly flat voice,

"Yes, you do look a bit drawn. You seemed lively enough ten years ago when I met you."

My encounter with Tsunoki ten years earlier had been at my wife's funeral.

"Lively?" I said, turning to look at him.

"Oh, sorry—of course, that was Keiko's . . ."

His voice had an insincere ring.

Keiko had been killed by a car. It wasn't a pedestrian crossing, but I'm pretty certain it was an accident. Not suicide, I'm sure, though there is just a shadow of doubt. I myself always look on it as a case of accidental death. If it had happened another ten years earlier, though, the doubt would have been a shade stronger. . . .

By now it was twenty-three years since the defeat. Twenty years before, we'd been twenty-three or so, and the world had been picking up the broken pieces. . . .

I stopped thinking at that point, and downed the whisky in front of me.

4

The woman sitting on my right was beginning to loll against me. Drinking with Tsunoki and his young companion, I'd struck up an acquaintance with a couple of women who were there together. I don't remember which side spoke to the other first. We were all a bit drunk.

The five of us left the bar and went to sit round the table in the corner. The women introduced themselves: Maki and Tae. They didn't work there, of course. They looked like a pair of ordinary, respectable girls.

"Let's see—you're Tae, aren't you?"

"Right. That's Maki there." The girl called Maki was in the seat directly opposite me.

"How old are you?"

"Twenty-two."

"That's very young," I said, and felt for her breasts through her dress. I was bold enough about it to be able to make out their shape beneath my palm. Leaving the hand where it was, I took a look at her face and found her mouth right there in front of me. So I brushed it briefly with my own lips and said, as though the action had marked the end of some ritual,

"Now change places with Maki, will you?"

I made Tae stand up and gave her bottom a light slap to send her on her way. Maki got up from the other side of the table and came and sat beside me in Tae's place. As she did so, I heard Tsunoki on my left proclaim in an irritable voice,

"And to think it was always he who never got on with women! More unpopular than anyone else, he was."

It wasn't only drink, I was sure, that gave his voice that raw edge. I privately agreed with this remark, but pretended not to have noticed it.

Even so, my behavior after that was an act for his benefit. I remembered the practiced way in which I'd handled Tae, and taking it as a model put my hand straight to Maki's breasts.

"Are you about the same age as Tae?" I asked, massaging the breasts under their covering of cloth.

"Yes, twenty-two."

"Just the right age for someone like me." The remark brought me up short, because I really believed what I'd said. Fifteen years earlier, when I was twenty-eight, I would have felt terribly old. The disparity in our ages would have disqualified me from going around with a girl of twenty-two.

At that point the man next to me spoke again.

"Not much of the old reticence there, I must say!"

"What's wrong—you mean our ages are too far apart?"

"It's not just that."

The conversation was beginning to get me down. I would probably have done better not to meet him, I thought, and made an attempt to pass off his little sarcasm.

"How about you, anyway—still scoring with the girls?"

"There's no 'scoring' about it. I just happened to be popular with women. Damned popular, I was."

My eyes were on his face. He had a thoughtful look. I'd half expected he might show a fleeting sign of pain, but it was as though the
effect of the drink had created in his mind a momentary vacuum,
into which an intense nostalgia for the past had immediately poured.

It occurred to me that if I asked now I might get a truthful answer.
Looking back at the past had its dangerous aspects, for both Tsunoki
and myself. And an ominous clot of memory had, in fact, stirred
inside me too.

Twenty years earlier, Toru Tsunoki had been twenty-three and
a promising young author. His style was sensuous and florid, and his
name was heard in association with phrases such as "astonishing
genius" and "mastery." I, on the other hand, was on the staff of a
third-rate popular magazine far removed from the circles that published his work. We'd both been among the founders of a small
literary journal, which had published the first of his work to attract
attention. Whenever we met after that, he would announce, purs-
ing his lips and enunciating rather indistinctly,

"I've been asked to write a story for—" (here followed the name
of some well-known magazine).

The very diffidence of his manner blatantly proclaimed his pride.
Before long, he stopped putting in an appearance at the meetings of
our magazine.

That wouldn't have mattered in itself. I may have felt envy—
jealousy, even—but after so long it should have been possible to
look back on that youthful episode with indulgence.

I married early. Twenty years ago, I already had a wife. One
night, coming home from the office, I noticed an unfamiliar silver
box standing on the dining table. A long, narrow, metal box.

"What's that?"

"Mr. Tsunoki came. Around two."

"Surely he knew I wouldn't be here?"

"That's why . . ."

It dawned on me.

"He came to see *you*, did he? This is his present, I suppose?"

"That's right. Candy."

"It's not like him."

I meant that Tsunoki was well known for being miserly. He was also well known as a lecher.

"I know. I was surprised myself. He's normally so stingy. . . ."

Her tone was mildly derogatory, but her expression was almost good-humored. Somehow, she seemed to be blaming me for not being in Tsunoki's position—for not, in short, being Toru Tsunoki.

"Did he make a pass at you, then?"

"I suppose you could call it that." She stopped, then added hastily, "Not that anything happened, of course."

"I've got to get my shoes mended. There's a nail through. It hurts."

"Your shoes? What a funny man! Suddenly to bring up a subject like shoes. . . ."

He'd gone along, the promising young author, knowing I wouldn't be at home. Around the same time, I myself was walking along the street on my way to visit an illustrator I knew. The house was a good way from the station, and a nail in my shoe had stuck into the underside of my foot at every step I took. I could still feel it.

A month later, Keiko announced that she was pregnant. Tsunoki's face, I must admit, flashed into my mind at the time.

"You'd better get rid of it. We're in no position to bring up a child just now."

She agreed without demur.

5

Now, twenty years later, as he sat in front of me apparently lost in recollection, I could have asked him all kinds of things. For example:

"That day, did you and Keiko . . . ?"

"Did we?" he might have replied. "Oh—you mean, did we have sex? Well . . . as a matter of fact, we did."

But however convincing the reply might seem, I would never really know the truth. Even if I did, what good would it do me?

We must have stayed silent for a while. The next thing I knew, Tsunoki was saying to Maki,

"This is the first time you've met this fellow, isn't it?"

"Yes, of course."

"Then why aren't you looking more wary?"

"But I know what kind of he is."

"Say, Nakata—" (that's my name, Shuichi Nakata) "this girl here says she knows what you're like. Tell me, what *are* you like, anyway?"

His voice had a touch of irritation.

"She doesn't mean anything complicated—she just knows I'm a writer. . . ."

I broke off, realizing my answer might only aggravate Tsunoki's mood. As I feared, he looked sourer than ever and began to get bitchy.

"What's the world coming to? The girl feels safe because she's heard he's a novelist!"

"You're awfully sarcastic," Maki said and turned to me. "I've noticed him here occasionally. Who is he?"

"Toru Tsunoki," I said, casting consideration for him to the winds.

Maki was only twenty: she could hardly be expected to know the name. It had made the headlines for two years or so, and hadn't been seen in print since.

Maki looked vague, then said,

"But it isn't you being a novelist that makes me feel so safe."

"Are you sure you're not just kidding yourself?" said Tsunoki. But without waiting for her reply he turned to me. "The fact is," he said, "there's something I wanted to ask you. Here, this is the kind of job I'm doing at the moment—" He handed me a business card. "The advertising business, as you see. We do the editing for a trade magazine, among other things. I'd like you to do something in instalments for it. Young Uda here'll be in charge."

It was his first mention of his young companion's name.

"Instalments? Serials aren't really my . . ."

My obvious reluctance concealed a feeling that it was going to be difficult to get out of it. Undismayed, Tsunoki pressed ahead.

"No, not a story. Nor a series of essays, either."

What then, I wondered, curiosity stirring.

"A diary," he said.

"I see. . . . But any diary I might write nowadays wouldn't be of the slightest interest. I sleep a lot, write a little—and there you have my day. The same old things, over and over again."

Tsunoki's mouth twisted slightly and the tip of his nose seemed to grow more pointed, giving him a spiteful look.

"So that's why they say a writer has no life of his own."

"Surely, repeating the same things every day is precisely what life today is all about. Isn't it the same with you?"

"You might say so, I suppose."

In spite of his reply, he looked as though he was not really convinced, but was holding himself ready to pounce at the first opportunity. It occurred to me that to talk was to lay myself open to attack, but I went on just the same:

"People talk a lot about the writer and 'action.' But if going big-game hunting in Africa constitutes action, then so does going to buy cigarettes at the little store on the corner; there's no essential difference. Is that the kind of thing you want me to write?"

"No, that's no good," he said firmly. "You're supposed to be an erotic writer, you see. Actually, only a certain proportion of readers think that; the rest see you as plain sexy."

"What's the difference between 'erotic' and 'sexy'?"

" 'Erotic' has class and 'sexy' doesn't. A very important distinction."

"I see."

I was still marveling over this when he went on,

"Someone once expressed the view that the sexual act was an infinite repetition of the same thing. What do you think?"

"From the overall point of view, it may be. But individual occasions aren't without their discoveries."

"Now, there I'm with you. Particularly in your case—you've been a bachelor for the past ten years, so I don't suppose you've stuck to one particular woman."

"In other words, that's the kind of diary you want me to write?"

"Correct."

"I'm not very tempted."

"There's no need to get all uptight about it. You can invent the entries."

I said nothing.

"Think it over," he pressed. "I'll get young Uda here to remind you about it."

And with an air of finality he turned to Maki and said,

"You *were* kidding yourself, weren't you?"

"No, I wasn't. I *know* what sort of man Mr. Nakata is."

"You mean, you both have some common acquaintance?"

The same suspicion had just occurred to me. But she said,

"No, that's not it."

I wondered exactly what kind of impression I'd made on her as a man. But it was Tsunoki who said,

"What sort of a man is he, then?"

"I can't say here," she replied.

"Where *could* you say?"

"If I was alone with Mr. Nakata. . . . But both of us have got people with us, so I can't tonight, can I?"

"I want to know what I'm like," I interrupted. "It needn't be this evening, but I'd like to be alone with you."

"All right," she said.

"Are you coming here tomorrow evening?" I asked Tsunoki.

"Tomorrow? No, not tomorrow."

"How about it?" I suggested to Maki. "Let's meet here tomorrow evening."

Seeing her nod, Tsunoki smiled faintly.

"That's the way, Nakata! If only you'd behaved like that in the past you'd have had more luck."

"I knew that all along. But it's the nature of youth not to be able to put what it knows into practice."

"*I* could, though."

Normally there's a great discrepancy between real women and womanhood as envisaged by a young man in his twenties. With Tsunoki, there'd been no such gap. Had he perhaps had a grasp of feminine nature beyond his years? He, at least, would have liked to think so. . . .

"*I* could," he said again, as though to drive his point home. I had an impression that he was talking about his relationship with Keiko. At the time, I'd been torn between belief and suspicion; when the candy in the silver box he'd brought was all gone, I used the box for a while as a pen-tray. I recalled Tsunoki's face in the days when he'd been an up-and-coming young author, and said,

"That was because you had confidence in yourself."

6

The following evening, I arrived at the agreed time to find Maki already there.

"Punctual, as I expected," she said. "I've been here quite a while. I'm a bit drunk."

" 'As you expected'?"

"That's the kind of man I thought you were."

"That's it—that's just what I've come to hear about."

"It's quite simple, really. It wouldn't take a moment to tell you. I could have told you yesterday, but . . . By the way, your relationship with that man—Tsunoki his name was, wasn't it?—seemed to be kind of involved."

"Is that how it looked to you?"

"I don't know in what way it's involved. But somehow it seemed as though you've made victims of each other."

She's pretty sharp, I thought, but asked with deliberate unconcern,

"Victims? You mean, we've hurt each other in some way?"

"That's not quite it. I can't say exactly. It's just that I felt I'd better not talk in front of him."

I stayed quiet, waiting for her to go on. After a short while she opened her mouth, but only to talk about something else.

"You behave yourself when we're alone, don't you?"

I looked at her, not sure of what she meant.

"Yesterday you touched my breasts."

"I was drunk, you know."

"Not all that drunk."

I wondered if I'd behaved that way for Tsunoki's benefit. With Maki, it may in fact have been so. But not with Tae. Or was it? No, it couldn't have been. . . . I was still unsuccessfully sounding out my true feelings when she said,

"It makes me throw up. . . . It happens to me occasionally, though never before with somebody I've just met . . . and it always makes me throw up."

"Throw up? But you weren't sick yesterday, were you?"

"That's just it. Usually, it makes me queasy just to sit next to a man."

"Do you feel queasy now?"

"Not a bit, that's the funny thing about it. That's why I wanted to be alone with you—to make sure."

"So that's why," I echoed, at a loss for anything better to say. There was a brief silence.

"You don't feel me as a man then?"

"I wonder if that's it?"

"Surely it's something in you, isn't it?"

"Yes . . . but I'm not sure, though. That's why it's so funny."

I studied the woman Maki with fresh eyes. Neither fat nor thin. Neither heavily nor slightly built. Almost no makeup. Judging from the sparkle in her eyes and the way she used them, she was neither lacking mentally nor particularly neurotic. If anything, you'd call it an attractive face. But the attractiveness didn't have anything sensual about it; it was the kind that comes from an alert mind, perhaps, or innate good nature. Her skin would have had a healthy tan if it weren't for a slightly leaden tinge, as though someone had brushed a film of gray over it. The texture wasn't particularly fine, either.

As a woman, she seemed a perfectly acceptable companion to talk with over a drink, as I was doing. But why should being touched by a man make her sick? Why should I be an exception to the rule? And was what she said to be taken at face value, at any rate? I began to be intrigued.

"Let's go," I said.

I got up, paid the bill, and we went outside. With Maki still at my side, I plunged into the back streets. I walked in silence; her failure to inquire where we were going suggested, almost, that she knew our destination already.

I came to a halt at the entrance to an inn, and her gaze went from my face to the lighted sign over the entrance, then back to my face again. As we passed in through the gate, I sensed her having a moment's hesitation behind me, but she followed me in all the same.

The maid showed us to our room and disappeared. She'd be back in a moment, bringing tea: an awkward gap, even for a couple who knew each other better than we did.

We sat facing each other on either side of the low table in the center of the Japanese-style room. Maki, somehow, had an air of steeling herself against something.

"Come on, relax!" I said. She tried to sit more naturally but only succeeded in looking more awkward than ever. She didn't seem to know what to do with her legs in their narrow slacks, and her hands moved about restlessly.

"Just let your shoulders slump," I said, smiling.

She gave an embarrassed little smile.

"Do you often come to this kind of place?" she asked.

"Sometimes. How about you?"

"This is my first time. And what do you do?"

"Do you have to ask?"

"Then what are you sitting there so still for?"

I smiled again.

"I believe it really *is* your first time. The next thing is that the maid brings us tea. . . ."

Before I'd finished speaking there came the sound of the sliding doors opening, and the maid appeared. As soon as she'd gone again, I got up, went over to Maki, and grabbing her arms hauled her up. She came to her feet, but without conviction.

"You're heavy," I said. "Stand up properly."

With another embarrassed little smile, she stood up under her own steam. Without releasing my grip on her arms, I dragged her bodily as far as the sliding doors that separated us from the next room.

Letting go of her arm with one hand, I opened the doors, revealing quilts already set out on the tatami. The room was so small that the quilts seemed almost to fill it.

Maki's body went rigid again.

Putting both arms around her, I tried to drag her into the next room. She struggled violently.

I'm not strong, but she was no match for a man. My arms still encircling her, I pushed her over onto the bed. At that moment I heard her blurt out, as she resisted for all she was worth,

"It's all wrong, all wrong."

"What's all wrong?" I asked, but she just went on muttering,

"It's all wrong."

"Do you mean this wasn't the agreement? But surely you know what kind of place this is, don't you?"

I put both hands in the waist of Maki's slacks and tugged downward with all my strength. Her panties slid down with her slacks, leaving her lower half completely exposed.

I found myself with my arms around her waist, pinning her lower half down with the weight of my own body, as she lay face up on the bed. My face was pressed firmly against her naked abdomen. But at that point her body went still. I raised my face slightly from her belly.

Directly before my eyes lay an expanse of naked flesh, and, more or less on a level with my chin, the black thicket at its base—a dense, vigorous growth. Since leaving my first youth behind, I've grown more and more fussy about women's bodies. I prefer pubic hair to be soft and downy.

I was about to disentangle myself when I caught a whiff of scent. I brought my face close to her naked belly again, but could smell nothing. I drew my face down her belly: no doubt about it, the fragrance came from the pubic hair.

It didn't go with Maki's type of woman. In fact, it was almost unnatural.

I lifted my head away, and something made me look around me. As I did so I caught sight of something gold and shining on the white sheet beside Maki's body. Sitting up, I picked up the shining thing between my finger and thumb. It was a short, sharply pointed, gold pin.

"What's the matter?" I heard Maki say. "Can't you make love?"

"Make love?" I echoed in a voice that must have let suspicion show through. Suspicion not of her words, but of the note almost of grief in her voice.

In silence I held out the golden pin for her to see.

"Oh!" She stretched out a hand and carefully picked the pin from between my fingertips. Our nails brushed lightly, and for a moment I felt we were linked together by a fine line. (Later, I was to recall the moment from time to time, and to wonder about this business of being linked by a line. I seem at the time not to have felt that we were "linked by a fine *golden* line," which might seem strange to some people, but I hardly have the kind of nature that sees men and women as linked by anything so romantic. . . .)

"Careful!" I said. "What's it for?"

Ignoring my question, she raised herself and seemed to be searching for something on the bed. Eventually, her fingers approached the sheet. They came up again and, held between them, I saw a small golden sphere. About the same size as the head of a small nail.

Sitting on the bed with her lower half still uncovered, she fumbled with the lobe of her ear and thrust the sharply pointed pin through it from behind. Then she fitted the gold ball onto the projecting point of the pin, and the result was an earring.

A sympathetic shudder ran through my body.

"Doesn't it hurt?"

"There's a hole in my ear, silly."

"When did you have them pierced?"

"Let's see . . . about a year ago."

An equivocal expression crossed her face as she replied, and she added as though trying to cover it up,

"They anesthetize the lobe, then punch a hole in it. Then they leave a thread through the hole, and you move it about backward and forward every now and then."

"What a revolting business."

"Now *that's* just as I imagined you. . . ." Quite without warning, she laughed. "But there's still something wrong."

"Was that what you meant when you said 'it's all wrong' a while ago?"

"Did I say that?"

"You did."

"I pictured you, you know, as thin, with a kind of tired curve to your back. . . . I wasn't very far out there. And you had a lot of gray hairs, and your wife was unfaithful to you, and you knew, but went on with your life quietly, without complaining. . . ."

"A typical girlish fantasy, in other words. That's not my own idea of myself, at least."

"No, and it's not correct, either—touching a girl's breasts straight off, and bringing her to a place like this only the second time you've met her. To tell the truth, I was beginning to think I didn't know what you were like any more."

"You mean it wasn't till I took your clothes off that you realized?"

"Right. The picture I'd built up of you in my mind was still too strong, and even when you brought me here, I still told myself it'd be all right somehow. But look at me now!"

Her words made me aware that her lower half was still exposed. A perverse desire stirred in me. I grappled with her again and, meeting a certain amount of resistance, put my arms round her waist and pushed her over.

I found my face pressed against her naked belly once more. It suddenly struck me as comic that after such a short interval we should find ourselves back in just the same position.

She struggled to free herself, and I tried to pin her down, but I couldn't get any strength into my arms. After a while she said,

"Let's call it a day."

Her words took the heart out of me. Physically, she'd only had a limited appeal for me to begin with. Yes, we'd better give up, I thought, and shifted away from her.

"But it's peculiar," she muttered. "I don't feel sick."

"Get your slacks on," I said.

"Now I don't know *what* you're like."

She stood up and with sluggish movements put on her slacks, keeping her eyes fixed on my face all the while. She probably thinks I'm impotent, I reflected. But I did nothing to disillusion her, switching to interrogation instead.

"You say it's strange not to feel nausea. If you ask me, though, it'd be a lot stranger if you actually were sick. Do you have the answer to that one?"

The subtle look that passed across her face didn't escape me. Pain, embarrassment, anger, remorse—all kinds of things seemed to be mingled there, but nothing definite.

She stayed silent.

"If you don't," I went on, "I think you should start digging around in your past."

Still she stayed silent. My own words rebounded on me. Keiko's face rose up in my mind, and Tsunoki's, and the shape of a human embryo. And I had a mental picture of my spermatozoa and Tsunoki's, enlarged as though under a microscope, swimming their way toward Keiko's womb. . . .

"I'm sick of going back into the past," I told myself, shaking my head as though to dispel the images floating before my eyes. "It's not necessary any more."

Maki and I left the place without further incident.

7

One day while I was out, I took the opportunity to drop by the publishers of a certain magazine and refer to their copy of *Who's Who*. "Refer to" makes it sound too much like a public library. In fact, I was in the habit of dropping into the magazine's editorial department from time to time, and I'd been aware for some while of the volume standing on a shelf with *Who's Who* inscribed on its massive spine, but hadn't been able to ask to see it with the right air of casualness.

There would have been no need to hesitate at a public library, but the matter wasn't important enough for a visit there. I made up my mind quite suddenly, as the large office building hove into view through the window of the taxi taking me home. Yes, I thought to myself as I got out of the car, today I'd finally get it cleared up. . . .

I got the people in the editorial department to let me have the book. I was turning its pages at a desk in the corner when one of the editors asked me if I was arranging a marriage for somebody. His tone was joking, with an undertone of seriousness.

"Who knows?" I replied, deliberately making an exaggerated move to hide the bulky tome with my body. My research wasn't the kind you could explain to people.

I found the name I wanted almost at once: Torao Uchiyama. Doctor of Physics, university professor, 52. Wife Yuriko, 48, daughter of Eizo Teramura. The latter was an authority in the same field, as *Who's Who* itself recorded, but this was no news to me.

Torao Uchiyama was a genius. At the age of twenty-three he had discovered some revolutionary new principle and been awarded a doctorate. He'd been unusually young for the honor, and the newspapers had made a great deal of it at the time.

He had also, though, been a man of ambition. His marriage to the second daughter of Eizo Teramura had been, in a way, a strategic move. By now he was a likely candidate for the directorship of some important organization.

The thing I wanted to find in *Who's Who* was whether Uchiyama and his wife had had any children.

As I foresaw, they had remained childless.

8

The year following Japan's defeat, while I was at college, I began to be affected by an odd set of recurring symptoms. They would attack me after I'd gone to bed, just as I was falling asleep. I would feel my body going gradually rigid till I was as stiff as a ramrod. Then, with tremendous force, it would swivel round through an angle of about eighty degrees. It didn't really move—it was a kind of half-waking, half-sleeping hallucination—yet the illusion of actually moving at a sharp angle was completely convincing.

The moment after the change of angle, I would hear a kind of subterranean rumbling drawing closer and closer. It came in through my feet, climbed up my shins and thighs, and my whole body began to tremble violently. Something—something massive, like a tank—was trying to pass through my body. Rusty red sparks showered through the darkness. Slowly, the roaring thing advanced from my belly to my chest, the trembling grew fiercer still, and as the roaring reached my heart, I thought "I'm going to die. . . ."

The feeling of impending disaster stayed with me for some time, but eventually the tank, with a clatter of its treads, emerged from my head; the trembling of my body stopped, my eyelids came unstuck from my eyeballs, to which they'd been glued fast, and my eyes opened. But the sense of crisis still hung obstinately about my body.

The diagnosis was "a mild nervous breakdown." The doctor said that a month or two's change of air, though not essential, would probably do me good.

In the summer vacation, an acquaintance arranged for me to go to a place in the country not far from a provincial town. It was a village of farmsteads, scattered about a narrow strip of cultivated land caught between some hills and a river.

The village was poor. The people who were to look after me were one of the older families there. The buildings that stood in the compound with its white-plastered wall were imposing enough in themselves, but the people living in them gave the impression of leading a frugal existence. A small, sturdily built outbuilding had been allotted for my use.

At mealtimes, I would go over to the main house and join the family at table. They were a prolific lot, with eight children ranging from a boy at middle school to a newborn infant. What with the crowd, and the smell of drying nappies or something going sour that hung about the place, I didn't much enjoy my meals. But the head of the family, a man in his forties, and his wife who was somewhat younger, seemed well disposed and—partly because of my novelty value as a university student from the big city—treated me kindly enough.

"Today, as a special treat, I'll do 'spectacles' for you," the wife would say in the tone of someone indulging in some unprecedented generosity. "Spectacles," which puzzled me at first, turned out to be a pair of fried eggs. It was rather an anticlimax, even though to use two eggs at once was quite an extravagance in those days. On the other hand, she'd serve sweetfish—for me, a real delicacy—without any fanfare at all. Unlimited sweetfish were to be had in the nearby river.

I spent my days dozing, reading, or climbing in the hills. I'd take a path leading up through one of the graveyards that dotted the lower slopes. The summits of the hills weren't very high, but you soon felt you were deep in the mountains. The branches of the trees closed in an arch over the narrow path, and speckled sunlight filtered down through the dense foliage.

One day, halfway up the path, I met a girl who came walking down on sluggish, unsteady legs. There was something abnormal about her. The plump body might have belonged to a middle-aged woman, but the face was that of a girl. As we passed each other, I took a closer look at her. There was something pale green and wet around her lips. A single stalk of grass was stuck in her mouth. She wasn't just holding it there, but was munching at it furiously. I couldn't tell for certain whether we'd looked at each other or not, for her eyes seemed to be covered with a thin white film that obscured their focus.

Walking on for a while after passing her, I came to a place where there was a small waterfall. The slope flattened out temporarily; it was as though I had climbed up the wrist of a giant hand and come out onto the palm.

I'd already decided that when I got there I'd take a short rest, then turn back. The descent took no time; I almost ran down. Once I was out of the woods, the view opened up suddenly. I could see the graveyard at the foot of the hills almost beneath my nose.

Suddenly, I halted in my tracks. I'd caught sight of the girl, tiny in the distance, walking close to the white plastered wall. This was unexpected. She ought to have been out of sight long ago; either she was a terribly slow walker or she'd been dallying on the way. But the word "dallying" didn't go with her at all. I had a mental picture of her squatting, pointlessly, in the road.

Still more unexpectedly, the girl passed through the gate with the tiled roof that broke the stretch of white wall.

She must be one of the neighbors' girls.

It was just about suppertime. I went down the hillside without taking my eyes off the gate. Before long, I was going through it myself. The girl hadn't emerged from it in the meantime.

I expected to see her standing in the entrance or sitting there on the edge of the veranda. But my expectation was betrayed, nor was she to be seen inside the house. The house was single-storied, with only three rooms, each of which must have covered more than sixty square feet.

As I took my place at the table, I had an urge to ask about her, but something inside me told me to stay quiet.

All of a sudden, I stopped eating, my chopsticks poised in midair. I felt sure I'd heard something stir above my head. But I checked the impulse to look up at the ceiling. I seemed to feel the husband's normally laughing eyes fixed sharply on the side of my face that was turned toward him.

In the end I put no questions. I didn't even check on the husband's expression.

That night, I dreamed about fireworks: jet-black fireworks, opening up like umbrellas in an orange sky. They went on bursting, one after another.

When I awoke, it was already morning.

The room was full of bright light. I was lying on my back inside the mosquito net. It was hot, and the sliding doors had been left open. If I turned my head to one side on the pillow, I could see the garden, the main house, and the inner side of the plaster wall without moving the rest of my body.

The wall was white. For the first time I realized that it was the whiteness of a newly plastered wall, neither yellowed by age nor a grubby gray. I recollected how the house had swallowed up a young girl the evening before, and fancied that the whiteness was fresh because they'd sealed the girl up inside it.

Right from the time I'd arrived in the area I felt there was something out of joint about the house. The garden had a pond and an expensive-looking rockery, with a gnarled pine and a small, moss-covered stone lantern standing by it. The pond looked as though it ought to contain large golden carp, but nothing stirred in the muddy water.

The murkiness of the pond and the newly plastered whiteness of the wall—suddenly, the lack of harmony had something sinister about it.

I turned my head back to its original position and lay with eyes open, wondering where the girl had disappeared to.

I gazed upward without seeing anything—looking into my own head, you might say. But suddenly the boards of the ceiling, seen through the mesh of the mosquito net, became clearly visible, just as the misty outlines of an image seen through a pair of binoculars abruptly come into sharp focus. I could see everything now: the grain, the small knots, the marks where resin had oozed out and hardened. . . .

I was beginning to reflect on the pointlessness of staring at a ceiling when I noticed something. The ceiling consisted of seven long planks laid side by side. Some distance above my head, I could see the six lines where plank adjoined plank, parallel to the line of my body as I lay there. I assumed at first that the seven planks ran continuously from one side of the room to the other, but after a while I noticed that the farthest plank on the right had a break in the middle. The break looked just about big enough to thrust a finger through. The wood of the ceiling as a whole was aged to a light gray-brown, but the part round the gap looked darker and grimier than the rest. Why should that one spot have got so grubby? The grayish-brown of the other parts was the kind of color you'd expect them to acquire naturally with age, but the grime round the slit gave the impression of being caused by human agency.

"You'd think it was grease from people's hands," I muttered without giving it any deep thought. But my own words brought me up with a jolt. I imagined myself thrusting the tips of four bunched fingers into the crack. Imagination becoming unsatisfactory, I stood up, undid the net and cleared it out of the way, then shifted the table to a point directly beneath the crack.

I got up on the table and, stretching up my arm, found that my fingertips easily reached the ceiling. I thrust them, closed, into the crack. I must have put some strength into them, for the board moved slightly, horizontally, and the gap increased a little in width. The board moved quietly, smoothly, as though on castors.

Suddenly I felt an unexpected weight on my hand. The board had started to descend on me. Hastily, I supported it with both hands. But it wasn't falling in a flat position; as I relaxed my hands, the end where the gap was had started to descend, pivoting on the other end against the wall. It became a long, narrow plank sloping up from the tatami to the space above.

The house, which looked so uncompromisingly single-storied, had a loft above the ceiling. Treading cautiously, I climbed up the board. For a moment I stopped with just my head thrust into the murky space beyond. The pervasive smell of mold suggested that no one had been in there for a long time. As my eyes gradually got used to the darkness I could make out the surroundings: an empty loft, with the bare rafters showing.

I noticed a naked electric light bulb suspended on a short cord from one of the rafters.

"I expect the bulb's gone by now," I thought and started up the plank again. It was a broad, low space in which it was impossible to stand upright. I pressed the switch, and the bulb unexpectedly filled the space with bright light. Sixty watts, probably. The same boards spread out to form the floor, but there was one tatami in the corner, with a book in a dark blue cover lying on it as though someone had flung it down there.

I went toward the book more or less on all fours. It was about the size of a weekly magazine but had a stout cover. Opening it, I found a text sprinkled with equations and signs. A calculus textbook.

I'd no idea why such a book should be there, but I felt I knew where the girl had disappeared to.

There must be a similar attic in the main building. The floor would probably be covered with tatami, and I doubted if it smelled of mold; but there, too, lack of space probably made it necessary to creep about bent almost double. The impression I'd had at supper the night before, of something moving overhead, hadn't been an illusion after all.

Even so, why should they have had to hide the girl? Judging from her appearance she was close to imbecility. I pictured to myself again the eight children crowding the supper table, and wondered if the number ought really to have been nine. Could it be they didn't want it known that one of their number wasn't normal?

Suddenly, a man's voice sounded from down below.

"What are you doing up there, Shuichi?" The voice, low but penetrating, conveyed simultaneous reproach and alarm.

Stepping deliberately, my face composed in an expression of unconcern, I came down the plank. I decided to take the initiative, and said,

"I've found a secret room."

The master of the house gave me a brief, searching look, then said,

"There's nothing secret about it. All the houses around here are built like that, they use the loft to store things—"

He got so far, when his gaze happened to fall on my hand.

"Hey," he exclaimed. "That book—"

I noticed for the first time that without realizing it I'd brought the dark blue book down with me.

"It was in the loft. It's a calculus textbook."

Even now, more than twenty years later, I can still see quite clearly the odd mixture of expressions that went across his face at that moment. I could make out pride, and hesitation, and something resembling regret. The regret, I'd say, was occasioned by having undertaken to look after a student like me.

Before long, the expression began to resolve itself, and the determination to make some important confession became apparent.

"I want you to keep this to yourself, but . . ."

"You don't have to tell me then."

I half meant what I said. I didn't relish shouldering responsibility for other people's affairs. At the same time, the other half of me was moved by curiosity. He gazed at me for a while, then in a rather milder tone went on,

"Does the name Torao Uchiyama mean anything to you?"

I knew the name, though I personally was studying the humanities. I remembered reading in the papers, about six months previously, that a certain well-known university had given him a chair at an exceptionally early age. (It was five years earlier still that the papers had reported his becoming a doctor of physics.)

"Oh, you mean the man who was made . . ."

"Right. And doctor of physics too, quite a while before that."

"Yes, I remember. A brilliant man, in other words."

"Correct. Well, he's my nephew. My real nephew, too, not just by marriage." A look of pride came into this face.

"Is he, now! Who'd have . . ."

"Quite. Who'd have thought it?" he echoed. "Who, indeed? . . ."

I observed the touch of indignation that came into his expression: probably, I reflected, occasioned by the contrast between himself, buried there in the country, and Uchiyama.

"No doubt about it, he's an extraordinarily able man. He's my nephew, and you can't blame me for being proud of the fact, can you?"

"I wouldn't dream of it."

I spoke with mock solemnity, trying to smooth some of the excessive intensity out of his face. Quite suddenly, though, without altering his expression, he spat out,

"But his methods are despicable! He just uses people."

Not understanding, I said nothing, so he went on,

"You saw yesterday, didn't you?"

"Uh?"

"You needn't pretend, I mean the girl. You must have thought there was something odd about her, didn't you?"

"Now you say so. . . ." I replied noncommittally.

"All right, all right, I know! But she's not an idiot. On the other hand, she's obviously not normal. *Retarded*, shall we say?"

I said nothing.

"She's Uchiyama's younger sister!"

Uchiyama's family, he told me, lived in the small town not far from the village. The father, another outstanding brain, was a professor at the university in the town.

Torao, the eldest son, had shown signs of genius at an early age. While still at primary school, he'd easily mastered the contents of the book on calculus I had in my hand.

The children that followed, however, were failures. In terms of intelligence, they could only be called feebleminded. They were farmed out in the village while they were too young still to attract much comment among the neighbors. It was as though Torao had sucked up all the intelligence that ought to have gone into the others.

"You said 'others,' didn't you?" I demanded.

"There's a younger brother. Older than the sister, though. We took him while he was still a baby too."

"And he's . . ."

"Yes . . . retarded, I suppose you'd call him. He can't see, either. The idea, of course, was not to let people know the other children had something wrong with them. But don't get the idea we deliberately hid them up in the loft. They *like* that kind of dark, confined place. The same goes for Torao; it's the one thing he has in common with them. That book you've got there, for instance—I expect it was Torao who left it there, one summer when he spent the vacation in the outbuilding. But there's something about him that doesn't fit in with the idea of a scholar. I mean, he carried the same deception over into his marriage. He got away with it, too. Luckily for him, the man from the inquiry agency came directly to me. The brother and sister were tucked away in the loft at the time, which was a good thing. I told him they were away on a trip. Not that he seemed to have the slightest suspicion of anything wrong. The two of them spend all their time telling each other in little voices how famous their brother is. They never get tired of it."

The moment he'd finished this long speech, his face showed signs of regret at having given away the secret. I stood up, nearly banging my head in the process. I had a vivid mental image of the brother and sister creeping about in that oppressively confined space, boast-

35

ing to each other about their brother. The effect was more than squalid; it was faintly sexual, too.

"You won't tell anyone, of course," he said anxiously. The look of regret still lingered.

From then on, I was careful not to stop eating whenever there were signs of life overhead. It made me self-conscious in using my chopsticks, and their movements would become artificial. I couldn't, of course, look up at the ceiling, and at the same time I seemed to feel the husband's eyes on my right cheek, so my head would go round to the left. That inevitably brought my gaze onto the wife, who always sat on that side.

Invariably, she dropped her eyes.

In the end I cut my stay to less than three weeks instead of the scheduled month. I left without ever seeing the girl again, much less the blind brother. But mentally I took away with me a vivid image of a man and woman crawling about, whispering to each other, in the shallow space above the ceiling.

You'd think my nerves would have suffered still further from this depressing experience. In fact, I was entirely free from those odd symptoms after my return to the city.

9

Twenty-odd years passed. Torao Uchiyama was a prominent figure in his field. His scheme had worked. Just so long as he didn't have a child. . . . Any new offspring might well be of extremely low intelligence.

It's an instinct, I suppose, for women to want children. Particularly if the prospective father is brilliant. I wondered, then, what he'd said to keep her satisfied over the past two decades or so.

It must have been relatively easy just after the end of the war. Since most Japanese were fed up with life at the time, the excuse that to have children would be cruel to the kids themselves found ready acceptance.

I have a magazine on my desk now. It's an unpretentious affair of few pages, rather like a scholarly journal. Sponsored in 1948 by the Psychology of Everyday Life Association, it's devoted to a collection of articles on prostitution, including a discussion with some of the women themselves. The women came from the red-light district at Shinkoiwa. The piece came up against the GHQ censors and wasn't printed until recently. The interviewers—T, O, and S— were all students of sexual mores. The contents of the discussion, besides being extremely interesting, strike me as telling one a great deal about life, so I'm quoting a section of it here:

O: Just one more question to end with. Anything out of the way you'd care to tell us about?

Kumiko: Out of the way? Let's see, now. . . . Yes—there was one interesting customer, remember? A woman.

Fujiko: Now, *there's* one I won't forget in a hurry! Short-haired, and got up like a man. . . . [Omission]

Kumiko: She came to me too. Exactly like a man. Briefcase, short hair, pants and all, and her shoulders held back like this. . . . [Omission] "Here—," she says, "what d'you want to go sleeping with niggers and white men for, they won't give you any peace. I'm a woman, and I can pay plenty—so it's easy money, right?" "Just to *sleep* with you?" I said. "Sure," she said. I was a sucker, I thought I was onto a good thing, so I went to bed with her. Well, I got what I asked for! . . . She was no different to a man. She knew all the right places, like playing with your tits and all the rest of it. She could've given most men a few tips, if you ask me. [Omission] I was sure she had a dildoe or something, but no—just her own body, woman-to-woman-like. . . .

T: Rubbing them together, I suppose?

Kumiko: Rubbing and *putting* together. You wouldn't believe it! *We* could never manage it, even if we tried. She could get them smack together.

T: What position exactly?

Kumiko: Position? Well, not on top. Nor on her side. Sort of *crosswise*. And they come together. Shook me, it did!

S: And she had an orgasm?

Kumiko: Right.

S: You too?

Kumiko: Now you're asking! [Laughter] But to tell the truth, I got a kick out of it too. When it was over she said, "Here, you'd better go and douche"! [Omission] And something else she said tickled me too. "Now who says I don't have a dick!" she said. "Where, exactly?" I said. "Up there in my belly!" [Laughter] She might have, at that. Otherwise I don't see how she managed it. [Omission]

(What follows is the most important point of the whole excerpt.)

Kumiko: In a way, though, she was lucky, having something to live for. You know, somehow we're not really living at the moment, are we? No pleasure, just nothing better to do. . . . I reckon it's better to have something like that, that you're *interested* in, isn't it?

Fujiko: What d'you mean, "not really living"?

Kumiko: I mean living just because there's nothing better to do.

Kumiko was about my own age. I wonder whether she's still alive? If she is, I wonder what kind of a life she's leading?

That state of mind that the prostitute, twenty years ago, described as "not really living" could be expressed in all kinds of other, different ways. Anyhow, I still have a lingering feeling somewhere that I myself am "not really living." If you feel that way about life, there's not much point in having kids. So I don't have any.

Sometimes, though, I wonder whether that attitude of mine isn't gradually getting out-of-date, whether "not really living" wasn't just a passing fad in the years following the defeat. . . . As the years go by, more and more people look at me doubtfully when I say I don't have children.

You hear the same kind of thing even when writers are alone together.

"I don't see how anyone without a wife and children can really understand life," a man at one such meeting once said deliberately within my hearing.

When I found from *Who's Who* that Uchiyama had no children, I rehearsed an imaginary conversation in my head:

"Children?"

"We're not having any."

Significant silence.

"You see, our family has a history of imbecility. . . ."

These days, that's the kind of reply that would be most likely to satisfy people. In fact, though, the only reason I could ever contemplate such an answer is that I'm a novelist. For Uchiyama, it would be out of the question. I wondered what reply he always kept ready for his wife and the people around him.

10

One night in mid-January, it started snowing. Outside the window, white shapes went dancing by. Even in my room something told me quite definitely that it was snowing, though I didn't imagine the flakes as they touched the ground would make enough sound to reach the ears of someone indoors. I sat working at my desk for hours on end, aware of it all the while.

I finally went to sleep in the early hours, and it was a little after noon when I awoke. The day was fine, the sky an unusual blue, and the earth, equally unusually, covered with snow. When I was a kid, we used to have more snowy days in winter than we do now. Or so I remember, at least. . . .

Getting up and going into the living room, I found my breakfast waiting. Yumiko, the young woman who acted as a kind of live-out housekeeper, wished me a belated good-morning.

Yumiko makes good coffee. After I'd had my simple Western-style breakfast, I took a second cup with me back to the study. Gradually the aroma filled the whole room.

Outside the window the landscape sparkled, snow-covered in the sunlight. Without warning, I heard Tsunoki's voice deep down inside my ear:

"I hear you're lying pretty low these days, though. Seems you don't even get around town much, eh?"

"I'm one of the lucky ones," I said aloud, to shove the voice into the background.

"Why?" said a voice down inside my ear, though I couldn't be sure whether it was Tsunoki's or my own.

"I can sleep late in the morning and still make a living."

"But don't you feel ashamed, when everybody else is up early and working?"

There was no mistaking Tsunoki's voice this time. But I was used to this kind of exchange. About ten years ago (though I can't for the life of me remember whether it was before or after Kei-ko's death), I visited a glass factory to get material for an article I was writing for a newspaper. I and the young reporter with me were kept waiting for a while in the second-floor waiting room. Going to the window and looking out, we saw a laborer, stripped to the waist, plying a shovel on the ground directly below. We watched the edge of the shovel slice powerfully into the earth, scoop up the black soil, and fling it far away. Over and over again, untiringly, the powerful muscles of arms and chest repeated the same, regular movements.

The young reporter turned to me with a sardonic expression and said,

"Could *you* do that, Mr. Nakata?"

"I couldn't, and I wouldn't want to," I shot back. "Nor," I went on, "do I imagine that he'd care to go on, day after day, sitting all by himself at a desk for hours on end."

I spoke aggressively. His lips moved, but nothing came out. Another victim of the student movement, I thought with a sense of futility.

"Look at us—," I reflected in the same vein, "this man, myself, everyone—each of us in his own way busily scratching around for several decades in the small space occupied by his body, only to disappear in the end. All of us, equally reduced to dust. . . ."

I spent the afternoon in a pleasant frame of mind. I worked at my desk or lay on the bed reading, and in no time it was nearly dusk. Patches of snow in the garden had melted, and the dark soil was showing through in places. The sky was turning to sunset, and clouds trailed in orange flakes against a background of pale blue.

"I'm one of the lucky ones," I murmured as though to reassure myself once more.

"Why?" This time the question came from inside me.

"Because I've no wife, and no kids."

I murmured it furtively to myself, alone in my own room. It wasn't something you said to others; most people almost certainly would start arguing back.

"No wife, but women. And things managed so that I don't get the urge to monopolize them."

Lying face up on the bed, I stretched my back muscles to their full extent.

"Free," I murmured.

There was a knock, and the door opened. Yumiko. Seeing me on the bed, she stayed standing in the doorway. She had a bundle of mail in her hand.

"The afternoon mail just came."

I stretched out a hand toward her without getting up off the bed.

"You know perfectly well it's OK," I said as she hesitated. "To get mixed up with you in that way would be asking for trouble."

She smiled, came closer, and handed me the bundle. An attractive woman.

"You can go home now."

"What about your dinner?"

"I'm going out, you don't need to get anything."

11

Going through my mail I found a magazine carrying a discussion between myself and A, another novelist of my own age. In such discussions I sometimes talk impulsively without thinking, so that later when I see it in print there are parts that make me wonder whether I ever really said such things. It was the same in this case.

Nakata: I agree that the novelist is always a sensitive person. But if he was too sensitive in every respect he just couldn't go on living, so in some ways he has to pretend to be tough. You, for example—if you were in a bar and found a fly in your brandy, what would you do?

A: I'd say nothing, just leave it there without drinking it. If they noticed it, so much the better; if they didn't, that's too bad.

Nakata: Myself, now—I'd fish it out, show it to my neighbor, then chuck it away and drink my brandy. I'm not gentleman enough to dispose of the fly unnoticed and finish my drink. At the same time, it's no real effort for me to drink it—which means, I suppose, that in that respect I really *am* fairly tough. It might be interesting to make a collection of novelists' funny little traits like that. The extremely sensitive traits and the extremely insensitive ones. . . . Take that fondness of yours for sleeping pills, now—does it mean that your sleeping habits were once very easily upset?

A: I'm just weak-willed; I can't give them up. I wonder why someone who can break with women can't make the break with a drug?

Nakata: Drugs don't have a will of their own, so comparison with the sexes isn't valid. To be comparable to drugs, a woman would have to be all sex organ without any brain.

A: In other words, drugs just give you a pleasant feeling. There's no need to do anything on your own side.

Nakata: You know—if you struck up with a cretin, the relationship might last a good deal longer.

A: You've got something there. Perhaps that's the ideal I'm after. . . . Yes, that's one possible solution. If one's going to get fed up with women who've got intelligence, they might be better without any brains at all.

Nakata: Ideally speaking, I think so.

Seeing that I didn't even remember saying it, I couldn't have meant it very seriously, but it struck me now that many a truth is spoken in jest. If you said publicly that the ideal woman was a sex organ with arms and legs, a majority of women would get furious, and the remainder would laugh scornfully at the so-called "male dilemma." Among the men, there'd be a lot who'd agree, yet you could safely assume that in many cases the anguish would be there just the same, under the surface.

My feeling of well-being began to dissipate considerably.

"Anyway, I'm attached to the solitary life. And there's nothing in my environment at the moment that threatens to disrupt this state of affairs. . . ." Even as the words went through my mind, they sounded a good deal more negative than the "I'm one of the lucky ones" and the "free" of a while back. I smiled ruefully as I drew the telephone toward me. To call a woman.

I heard the phone ringing down inside the receiver, then almost immediately a female voice said,

"Hello?"

"Takako?"

"Speaking."

The tone of voice showed she knew who was calling.

"Work finished?"

"Mm."

Takako lived in a single-room apartment, where she taught flower arrangement during the day as a way of making ends meet. I visited her there about once a week. The relationship had been going on for four years now. The words "flower arrangement teacher" might suggest a middle-aged woman, but Takako wasn't yet thirty. Her body was small-boned and slender, but mature in every way. Her skin had the whiteness of milky glass. She was the introspective type, and was always a bit embarrassed at first, but once that stage was past she let herself go with a vengeance.

"I'll be round, OK?"

"Right." Normally we hung up at that point, but not today. "I'm tired," she added. "I think maybe I've caught a cold. . . . But don't worry, I'll manage somehow. . . ."

"You don't have to 'manage.' You'd better get to bed early."

Replacing the receiver, I immediately started dialing another number.

"Hello?"

The woman's voice was husky, almost cracked, and I had an unpleasant foreboding.

"Can you get away this evening?"

As I'd expected, the voice came back,

"I'm not very well."

The voice sounded half-choked and breathless, as though her actual words might shatter at any moment and emerge as other, totally different words.

Not long after I'd struck up with this woman Natsue, she told me of her own accord that she had a rich lover. She lived in an apartment in a ferroconcrete block not far from the downtown area, and showed no sign of having a regular job, so I'd already more or less put two and two together. It didn't bother me at all: I preferred relationships between the sexes to have a strong sporting element in them.

When she confessed the truth to me, I asked just one thing.

"This lover of yours, he comes to your place, I suppose?"

"That's right."

"So if someone calls you and there's no answer, it sometimes means you're out and sometimes that he's there with you, does it?"

I had a mental picture of the phone ringing to no avail beside two naked, intertwined forms.

"No," she replied. "The only time I don't answer is when I'm out. Incidentally," she went on, speaking rather more rapidly, "when there's no answer, how many times do you let the phone ring?"

"An interesting question. The answer tells something about the person's character." I took my time over the words. "Let's see— around five or six times, say?"

"Just as I thought. I'm the same, I always give up myself after five or six rings."

I fixed one of her eyes with mine and said in the same unhurried tone,

"You gave something away just now, didn't you?"

"Uh?"

For a moment, she obviously considered bluffing. Then her expression showed she'd given up the idea, and with a thin smile she said,

"Gave myself away? . . . How, though?"

"You always answer, then, even when your lover's there with you?"

"Yes."

Her expression this time was clearly resigned to the inevitable.

"No matter what you're up to?"

"Yes."

"You get a kick out of it?"

"No—it's him, he's peculiar. 'Go on, answer,' he says. Then he deliberately bounces around on top of me."

"Does he know you have relations with other men?"

"I'd say he half trusts me and half suspects. Sometimes the things he says make me think he suspects. I always deny it. If he found out, there's no telling what would happen to me. He's that kind of man."

12

I'd only known Natsue for a few months, but so far, though I'd sometimes got no answer when I rang her apartment, she'd never answered and then refused my suggestion.

"Can you get away this evening?"

"I'm not very well."

To continue the conversation would only prolong her lover's fun. Even so, if I hung up immediately it might make him suspicious. I ventured another word into the receiver.

"No go?"

"Stop it!"

Somehow the words didn't sound like a simple reply to me. With a fierce clatter, the phone was cut off at the other end.

"I see. . . ." I muttered to myself as I slowly replaced the receiver.

In a way, the muttering was itself a sign that I was upset. A vision of Natsue's naked body came into my mind. It was very like Takako's. Takako's breasts were a bit larger, and Natsue's skin was a light amber. But the one big difference was that Takako's body would dwindle and melt away in your arms like a snowflake in the palm of your hand, whereas Natsue's body got more and more supple, with a kind of inner resilience, and faintly damp all over with sweat.

I had a mental image of a man's broad, bare back covering Natsue's nakedness. Natsue's knees were drawn right up, and I could see the hollows behind them, wet with sweat. . . .

Here—I demanded of myself—what's bugging you? I'd had no intention of monopolizing her, even in the beginning, yet my mind was raw and smarting just the same. It felt remarkably like jealousy. Probably the scene my imagination had come up with had been a bit too strong to take. Natsue might well have been getting the same perverted pleasure as her lover while she replied to me, holding on tight to the receiver. Cooperating, in other words, with the man lying on top of her. . . .

That was what I didn't like about it. As A and I had agreed in our discussion, I'd have felt a great deal easier about it if Natsue had been an idiot.

Even so, along with the pique, there was a sensible urge to cut my losses. I knew a certain inn where I'd once been a regular, though I hardly ever went these days. If I went now, I could easily get them to call a girl for me. That way, I'd almost certainly get rid of my grievance.

After all, Takako, Natsue, and the unknown call girl were all on the same level so far as I was concerned, weren't they?

I started getting ready.

The taxi was drawing close to the inn I was heading for when I happened to notice the scenery outside the window. We were just passing through the street with the bar in which I'd met Tsunoki and Maki.

"Right—this'll do here," I told the driver, and got out.

There were many places on the ground round about "Loco" where the snow hadn't melted. I thought of Maki: yes, she was just the sort of girl who'd come out on a night like this.

She wasn't there. Seating myself at the bar on a tall stool, I'd finished my first whisky when a young bartender in a white coat came up and said,

"Why, it's Mr. Nakata, isn't it? Would you like me to give Maki a ring?"

I hesitated for a moment, feeling as though he'd been eaves-dropping on my private thoughts, then recovered and said casually,

"Good idea. Would you?"

I could hear him phoning at the other end of the bar.

"Hello? Matsue from 'Loco' here. Is Maki in, please?"

A brief exchange, and he was back facing me again.

"They say she left a while ago. They don't know where she went, so she may be along here, who knows?"

"Right. Thanks. Who was it answered, then?"

"Her kid sister."

" 'Matsue'—that's a girl's name, isn't it?"

"Oh really!" He giggled, covering his mouth with one hand in an effeminate gesture. "My first name's Yuzuru. Matsue's my sur-name."

"What does the name of this place—'Loco'—mean?"

"No special meaning so far as I know. I suppose somebody just took a fancy to the sound of it."

When I got home after my first visit—the time when Tsunoki had fetched me there—I'd looked the word up in an English dic-tionary. I'd a feeling I might find it listed as an abbreviation for "locomotive," but I was wrong. What I found in fact was "loco: the locoweed; or, a brain disease affecting domestic animals poisoned by the weed." But I kept quiet about it now, and asked another question instead.

"What's Maki's connection with this place?"

"She's a customer, of course. Why? . . ."

"Nothing. It's just the informal way you called her."

"But she's one of our regulars."

Yuzuru's gaze switched to the entrance.

"There—you see!"

The door was just closing behind Maki. She saw me immediately and came up. Instinctively, I looked down at her feet. The tips of her white boots were wet and dark with mud.

She sat down next to me and said, with her eyes on Yuzuru,

"I love snowy days."

"I called your place just now, to tell you Mr. Nakata was here." She turned to me.

"Well, I'm glad I found you. It must be three weeks by now. What did you do over the New Year?"

"Stayed in bed."

"A cold? . . ."

"No, I just slept."

I was lying. Since the beginning of the year, I'd seen Takako and Natsue twice each. "Seen" means "slept with." Not "slept." Sometimes, even, we exchanged almost no words other than those necessary to the business in hand.

Speaking of lies, Takako believed I had a wife and children. I hadn't really lied to her, though; she'd talked herself into it. A few times after we'd first started having physical relations, she'd said to me in a diffident little voice,

"I could give you a spare key if you like. . . ."

Something about me must have looked embarrassed, for she went on immediately,

"But then, you wouldn't want the key to get a life of its own, would you?"

An interesting way of putting it. But I said nothing.

"The more you look for somewhere to hide it," she continued, "the more it seems to come alive, doesn't it?"

At this point I realized her error. The reason for my awkwardness had been a feeling that to accept a key would be like allowing her to impose a small, ever-present second self on me. But I didn't care to correct her mistake.

I behaved in line with her misconception. For one thing, I made a point of never staying at her place.

"I don't like novels," she once said. "I don't even read yours."

On another occasion, she said,

"I saw a photo of you in a magazine I was looking at in the hairdresser's. All alone. You don't seem to like being photographed with your family, do you?"

"No. Cosy family groups bore me to tears."

You couldn't really say that my reply was a lie, either.

"Things are easier for me that way," she would say—and sometimes a sudden doubt would strike me. I'm sure that at first she'd been perfectly sincere. But it was four years by now. Sometimes a suspicion brushed my mind that she was perfectly aware of everything. For all I knew, she might have found out, and been playacting her error ever since.

13

So I was sitting at the bar in "Loco," having given up the idea of going to the inn for a call girl. In place of a woman who sold her favors, I had Maki. In the circumstances, I couldn't help viewing Maki in terms of the pleasure her body was likely to confer.

Unfortunately, as on the previous occasion, she just didn't get to me at the physical level. All the same, I had a strong presentiment that I'd end up taking her to bed.

Just once I tried defying the presentiment.

"How's the nausea tonight? . . ." I whispered in her ear.

"None, I think."

"How come?"

"I wonder. . . . Maybe it's just my preconceived idea of you."

Maki's "idea" was that in my case the aura of masculinity wasn't too overpowering. But that notion should have been dispelled on the last occasion I met her. I said nothing, so she went on, in a light, playful voice,

"A riddle, aren't I! Like 'A hill full, a hole full . . .' "

" 'A hill full, a hole full,' eh?" I said. "That's from *Mother Goose*, isn't it? Not," I added, "that I remember any of it myself."

There's hardly a phrase either of poetry or fiction that I could quote from memory.

"Well!" she exclaimed. "Who'd have thought you were interested in things like that!" Her eyes lit up, but her voice was bantering. "I know a lot of them by heart." And in a small voice she recited:

> "A hill full, a hole full
> Yet you cannot catch
> A bowl full."

"What's the answer?"

"Mist, silly."

"Mist? Well, that's a good straightforward answer, at least. I only wish things were as simple in your own case."

She stayed silent, eyes fixed, face expressionless (though "expressionless," of course, is a kind of expression in itself). Getting back to the subject, I said,

"But isn't the rhyme you just quoted a bit dull? No cruelty."

"Yes . . . I suppose you're right. Most of the *Mother Goose* stories are dreadfully cruel, but the riddle verses aren't like that."

"I wonder why?"

"Yes, I wonder. . . . Though what makes me wonder more is why so many children's stories and songs in other countries should be so cruel. By the way, do you know this one?—"

"Hold it! Have you always known the words of so many children's rhymes by heart?"

"No, I read them and learned them all in the past six months or so."

And in a still smaller voice than before she recited:

> "Pease porridge hot,
> Pease porridge cold,
> Pease porridge in the pot,
> Nine days old."

She raised her left hand, fingers outspread, in front of her face. The fingers—slender and flexible, with barely noticeable joints—were a surprise to me, knowing Maki's body as I did. With the index finger of her right hand, she pointed to the thumb of her left:

> "I gave this one some."

Next, she lightly pressed the index finger of her left hand with the same finger of the right, then moved on to the middle finger and ring finger in turn. As she went, she recited:

> "I gave this one some.
> I gave this one some.
> I gave this one some."

And as she reached the little finger:

> "Little finger, little finger,
> Didn't fetch any water.
> Didn't carry any firewood.
> Didn't make any porridge.
> So I won't give any to *you*!"

"I see. Where's that one from?"

"It's a Russian children's song. Or rather, it's a thing they sing while they're playing some kind of game."

I'd been watching Maki's face in silence. Now I said, in a voice as quiet as hers,

"And you, I suppose, are the little finger?"

I didn't mean anything very special. But neither was the remark entirely uncalculated. As I sat silently watching her face, every detail of her behavior and mine three weeks earlier passed through my mind and disappeared again in a series of brief flashes. Maki and myself going into the inn room together. Maki lying back with her lower half completely exposed. Myself with my face shoved against her naked belly. Maki's dense, luxuriant clump of hair. The whiff of perfume that drifted up from it. Maki and I, eventually, leaving the inn still innocent of each other's flesh. . . .

But her eyes went serious at my remark. For a while she in turn watched my face in silence.

"It's no use," she said finally. "I'll have to find some definite answer."

"To the question of why you don't feel sick? Or the question of why you do?"

"That's right—to both." She drained the whisky in her glass in one gulp. "Will you help me find it?"

She got down from her stool and stood there.

"Shall we go?" I said.

Outside, we set off side by side. From time to time I could feel the snow crunch beneath the soles of my shoes.

We both knew where we were going. The same inn as before.

"You know what litmus paper is?" I asked her abruptly as we walked. She looked up at me doubtfully.

"It turns red in acid and blue in alkali," I went on, "—or is it the other way round? I forget—after all, I was still at middle school when I learned about it."

53

No response.

"That's what I feel I am—a piece of litmus paper."

Maki dropped her gaze and giggled.

Once we were in the room, I kept her standing and, pressing her up against the wall, slowly removed her garments one by one, beginning with her coat. I stripped her where she stood, rather roughly, as though my hands were peeling off layers of skin. I knew very well that most women preferred it that way.

I took the usual precautions. Physically, as I'd expected, she was low-key. Her body didn't move; she just twisted her head from side to side on the sheet, violently and continuously, so that her hair flopped about wildly.

"D'you feel sick?"

As I said it, the movement of her head became more violent still, then gradually slowed up again.

"OK?" I ventured. Again the movement of the head stepped up. Not a word came from her, from beginning to end. First her right ear would appear beneath my eyes, then the left. The small golden balls that clung to them flashed and disappeared. The lobes seemed rather flushed; they reminded me of a spoiled child shaking its head when it refuses to do what it's told.

After I detached myself, she lay where she was for a while, then opened her eyes, which had been tightly shut, and said,

"I did it, didn't I? With a man."

"With a man? . . ."

As I repeated the words, puzzling over their significance, something flashed into my mind. The scent I'd noticed on a certain part of her body.

"You mean, that with a *woman* you . . .?"

If Maki was interested in lesbianism, then it explained the mystery of the scent.

"That's right."

There was something noncommittal about the affirmation.

"But you don't mean this is the first time you've been to bed with a man?"

She said nothing, her expression as equivocal as ever. Almost instinctively I looked for bloodstains on the white sheet. Not that I thought absence of bleeding necessarily meant the woman hadn't been a virgin. No marks of blood; but Maki's equivocal attitude still bothered me.

"Are you pleased, then, that you managed it without the nausea getting in the way?"

" 'Pleased'?"

This time there were signs of slight annoyance.

"But surely it means you're better, doesn't it?"

" 'Better'? Oh, come off it!"

Maki had dropped her vagueness for a look of frank indignation.

"Why 'come off it'?"

"Well, for someone who writes novels to say such a thing. . . ."

"But surely you're what they call a lesbian—I mean, a pervert?"

I was being deliberately provocative, hoping to shake her into showing what lay behind the noncommittal pose.

" 'Pervert,' he says! You don't have the faintest idea! A man and a woman together's quite different from two women. It's another dimension altogether."

"Oh, I see. Personally, I wouldn't know. I had an idea that a woman turned to other women because getting hurt by a man in the past had stopped her from having normal relations with the other sex. If it's a different dimension, then I've got a lot to learn."

I felt secretly relieved as I spoke. What Maki had just said meant that she could be kept at the edge of my life and not allowed to become a burden.

"Well, seeing that my role as a piece of litmus paper is over," I said, eyes on her face, "we can just be friends from now on, right?"

She met my gaze and her lips parted, but nothing came out.

14

I'd only just awakened when the call came, so my brain must have been rather fuddled. The caller identified himself as Uda and said something about a piece I'd promised to write, but I couldn't place him immediately.

"Mr. Uda? Where exactly—?"

"About a month ago—I was introduced to you by Mr. Tsunoki."

Of course, I remembered now: Tsunoki had asked me to write something for serialization in a trade journal he was connected with. He'd wanted a diary—a fictional one would do, he'd said. But the subject had come up in the course of idle conversation in the bar "Loco." I'd no recollection of agreeing, nor any intention of doing so. I said as much over the phone.

"But," said Uda, "Mr. Tsunoki said I would remind you about it, surely?"

"I believe he did, now you mention it."

"Anyway, I'd be grateful if I could see you at least. Perhaps I could drop round now?"

Even if Uda came alone, the figure of Tsunoki would be hovering in the background, following him into my house. I found the idea rather depressing.

That day, I was due to go to a general hospital in the center of the city for my twice-weekly allergy shot. I arranged to meet Uda in the waiting room of the Department of Internal Medicine.

It was a big hospital. The door leading to the department lay straight ahead from the front entrance, with the entrance to the Pediatric Department on its left. Rows of plain benches stood in the rather spacious area between the two entrances. I went into the treatment room, had my shots, and came out to see a young man with a familiar face sitting on a bench that stood against the wall a little apart from the rest. I went up, greeted him, and sat down at his side.

"This hospital doesn't smell of disinfectant, does it?" Uda remarked without preliminaries.

"I wouldn't imagine you're very closely acquainted with hospitals."

"Actually, I was pretty unhealthy as a kid. The smell of disinfectant has all kinds of associations for me."

"I imagine you mean cresol. There's none of that here, I agree. Methods of disinfecting must have changed."

"It was a depressing kind of smell. . . ." he said. "But then," he added, his gaze flicking about him, "there's something depressing about all hospitals."

"What do you expect?" I said. But he had something else on his mind.

"Is it part of your strategy, for us to meet in a place like this?"

"Strategy? . . ."

"To help you refuse. After all, there's quite a difference between the kind of thing we want you to write and the atmosphere of this place."

"I see. . . . You seem to be pretty shrewd for your age. Actually, though, that hadn't occurred to me. I just thought it would be more convenient for you here, being close to your office. . . ."

And I was about to launch into my refusal when a young woman wearing a brown coat passed directly in front of us with a dark green bundle in her arms.

A long, narrow stand stood against the wall opposite. Its flat top was covered with white cloth and supported, at about the height of an adult's chest, by four iron legs. It looked like the kind of trolley used for moving patients about, except that the legs didn't have castors. I wouldn't have scrutinized it so closely, though, if the young woman hadn't deposited the green bundle casually on top of it and disappeared.

I gazed at the bundle there on the stand without giving it any special thought. The bench we were sitting on was close to the entrance of the Pediatric Department, and only nine feet or so separated us from the opposite wall. In fact, I was not really gazing at the bundle; it was simply registering itself on my line of vision.

Suddenly, the bundle moved. Like an enormous caterpillar, it lay there silently wriggling. At one end, the color of flesh appeared through the thin green cloth.

An exclamation escaped us both simultaneously.

"Do you think that's a baby?" I said.

"It'll fall if it's not careful."

Uda moved as though to get up. It was a concrete floor. Without stirring I went on, my eyes fixed on the still wriggling bundle,

"Perhaps she put it that way because she knew it wouldn't fall."

If it dropped on the floor, I reflected, it could easily break its skull. But I felt no urge to get up off the bench. Somewhere my brain was thinking: that young woman didn't go through the entrance to the Pediatric Department—she turned off to the left, in the direction of the elevators. The area round the corner was out of our range of vision.

The bundle stopped moving, and Uda, who twice had half risen to his feet, sank back into his seat and turned to look at me.

"They say you don't like babies, Mr. Nakata," he said. "You've made up your mind never to have kids, haven't you?"

"Tsunoki told you, I suppose?"

"Yes."

"You—are you single?"

"Yes, but when I get married I want two, a boy and a girl."

All's right with the world, I thought. People nowadays had the leisure to think years ahead. Not that there was any guarantee it wouldn't all go up in smoke; there were any number of danger signals, if you cared to look for them. And yet even I—though admittedly in a different way from young Uda—was thinking way ahead into the future. There was a time when I was young when we were raided by American bombers every day for days on end. You weren't even sure you'd be alive to keep the next day's date, much less plan for marriage. I wondered just how far, and in what ways, those experiences during my formative period had left their mark on my outlook. . . .

"For your own sake?"

The question seemed to take him by surprise. I'd intended it as a continuation of our conversation, but the time I'd spent on my own reflections seemed to have broken the thread, so I rephrased it.

"I mean, do you want to have kids for your own sake?"

"Well . . ."

He thought for a while, with an expression as though he hadn't expected that particular question, then said finally,

"I suppose you might say so."

"I wonder how the kids feel, though, being born into a world like . . . Though being alive doesn't seem to bother *you* very much, does it?"

"How about yourself, Mr. Nakata—do you wish you hadn't been born?"

"That's a difficult question. Maybe it's partly due to not being very strong physically, but . . ."

"Mr. Tsunoki told me to find the answer. I mean, about why you don't want children."

I wondered where I'd heard something similar. Almost immediately I remembered: from Maki. "It's no use, I'll have to find some definite answer," she'd said, adding, "Will you help me find it?"

"To get down to business, though," said Uda, suddenly turning formal. "About the diary—since you seem to have collected quite a lot of material, there'll be no need to make it up."

"Is that another of Tsunoki's ideas?"

"No, it's partly my own."

They must have got wind of me and Maki at "Loco." I was silent for a while, so Uda went on,

"This next bit does come from Mr. Tsunoki, but he said that if you didn't feel too keen, it could be written for you."

"*For* me? You mean, by Tsunoki himself?"

"Well, yes. Personally, I feel that's going a bit far, but . . ."

I was just beginning to feel annoyed when quite suddenly my mood changed. I'd become curious to know just what interpretation Tsunoki put on my relationship with Maki, or on Maki herself.

"Let me think about it," I said. "Perhaps you'd call me again in a few days, would you?"

As I got up, the baby on the stand began to wriggle silently again. The stand was narrow, but the bundle lay on it diagonally, so it didn't seem in any danger of falling onto the concrete floor.

"Do you think it's been abandoned?" whispered Uda, who'd got up with me.

"Quite possibly," I said, though the suspicion hadn't crossed my mind till he spoke. I recalled the casual movements of the young woman, as though she'd been putting an ordinary package down.

"Yes, it's quite possible," I reaffirmed, as though to myself. And leaving Uda still wavering, apparently reluctant to go, I went out of the hospital.

15

I mulled over the question in the taxi on my way home. Could a woman abandon a child in the same casual way that she'd leave a parcel somewhere?

It made me remember something relevant.

It had flashed into my mind quite suddenly. A fragment of conversation I'd had with a woman in a bar, five years earlier:

"A friend of mine had a baby," she'd said. "The trouble was—"
(What followed I can't remember: whether the man walked out on her shortly after the baby's birth, or whether the baby was deformed, or whether she'd meant to have an abortion but had kept on putting

it off until it was too late—I've a feeling she said it was one or the other of the three.) "So she left it lying in a corner of the room without feeding it or even giving it a bottle."

I said nothing.

"It went on crying for three days, she said."

"And then?"

"Then it died."

At this point, I remember clearly, I took a good look at the woman's face. I did so because, to judge from the way she spoke, she might have been relating some perfectly commonplace, every-day matter. I don't remember what went before and came after this exchange. But her tone was utterly casual; she might have been telling me, for example, that the neighbor's cat had had four kittens.

I can't believe that a woman (at least, one in a normal mental state) would so casually abandon or kill a child she herself had given birth to. Could it be simply that extreme stress made her action *look* casual to the outsider?

But what about the bar hostess who told me the story? She was young, bright, and attractive; I remember her face quite clearly, though she's not at that bar any more.

There was something I couldn't put my finger on in my own thoughts as I sat in the swaying cab on the way home. As soon as the driver had put me down in front of my house and I got to my own room, I set about searching through the piles of magazines on my desk.

I'd remembered seeing something in one of them that had a bearing on what I'd just been thinking.

I soon found the number I wanted. Part of it was devoted to a special feature entitled "The Sacred Mountain of Osore." The ar-ticle was accompanied by a piece written by the novelist O, who comes from Aomori and is familiar with the mountain. It was this that I was looking for, and I quote part of it here:

Mt. Osore (Fear) is a corruption of the original name Usori. In ancient times, this mountain at the northern extremity of Japan's main island was a volcano that belched fire into the grim northern skies, spewing lava and raining down ash that blanketed the land like snow.

Its activity finally ceased, leaving only a sulphurous vapor creeping over the ash-covered surface of the earth, turning everything about it into a pallid waste. No wonder that men saw the place as a world of the dead, as Hell itself. . . .

The people there in the extreme north of Honshu believed that the spirits of the dead gathered at Usori. It became a sacred spot, and a popular cult grew up around the place. Every year, on the festival day of Jizo—the twenty-fourth of the sixth month by the lunar calendar—large numbers of pious men and women would come to the Entsuji temple on the mountain. Here and there in the temple grounds, groups of them would gather about mediums, shedding tears at the sound of the voices the mediums summoned up from the world of the dead. They firmly believed that the voices they heard were really those of their lost parents, husbands, wives and children.

In the summer of 1965 I joined N, a television director with Tokyo Channel 12, in presenting a scientific documentary program, part of a series entitled "Challenge to the Future," in which we went into the riddle of these mediums.

To state our conclusion first: the mediums were a kind of unemployment relief project necessitated by the poverty of northern Honshu.

Winters are long in the north. For the people who live there, with no other sources of entertainment, conjugal intimacies are the one thing that makes the long winter evenings tolerable. The result is children and more children: the chronic fecundity of the poor. Children there are seldom born because they are wanted.

It was not so long ago that the people of Aomori would refer to any thin, seedy-looking children as "the silk strain." As the family increased in number, the husband, in the absence of such civilized amenities as the condom, would bind a piece of silk round the tip of his member before having intercourse. Naturally, there was little hope of preventing pregnancy by such means, and the children—born, as it were, through the silk—were known as the "silk strain."

How did *they* feel, these children—were they happy just to be alive? Or were they miserable? . . .

A married woman who didn't want any more children would close her thighs *almost unconsciously* [my italics: Nakata] while giving birth. Thus the baby who had just put his head out into the world was promptly strangled. This practice, which was known as *tsubushi*, also survived until not so very long ago.

Even children who were not disposed of in this way had a hard time surviving amidst such poverty. [Omission] The insanitary conditions that were a joint product of poverty and ignorance encouraged the spread of eye diseases. A considerable proportion of babies who were not only born alive but actually survived were fated to go blind. Particularly unfortunate were blind girls, who could do no work and thus could not be married off.

Parents with such daughters would apprentice them to a medium. The blind girls (and they had to be apprenticed before their first menstruation, it was said, or the training would have little effect) underwent rigorous instruction in the techniques of spiritualism.

The phrase "almost unconsciously" which I've italicized in the above quotation is nicely chosen. The deed wasn't done "as though unconsciously"—i.e. with feigned unawareness—nor was it done "completely unconsciously." At the back of the pregnant woman's mind was one idea: that another child was, economically, unthinkable. So at the very moment when the baby looked out into the world, her body would contract—and the baby would be strangled. That, it seems to me, is the only correct way to interpret it.

When all's said and done, the unborn child invariably takes second place to the circumstances of the parents. In northern Honshu, "circumstances" meant poverty, but even in today's typical middle-class urban home *tsubushi* still survives. Some individual exceptions apart, two or three children are considered the ideal number in building a family. The rest are subjected to *tsubushi*. The methods, of course, are less primitive than they were up north: nowadays, we resort to devices that prevent the union of ovum and sperm, or to curettage in the early stages of pregnancy.

16

Sometimes I would call Takako, sometimes Natsue, depending on how I felt at the time. Where Takako was always shy at first, then gradually lost her reserve, Natsue would behave from the beginning as though she'd never heard the word modesty.

That day, it was Natsue I called.

"Why don't you come to my place?" she said.

"Wouldn't that be awkward for you?"

"Not a bit. He's away in Hokkaido on business."

I hesitated, so she went on,

"If there should be a call, it'd be better if I was at home."

The door of the apartment opened onto a combined dining-kitchen, with a Japanese-style living room beyond.

In the living room, I stayed standing, gazing round at the layout of the apartment.

"What's wrong? You look restless."

"Not particularly. . . . The bedroom's through there, is it?"

"That's right."

I shed my overcoat and sat cross-legged on the tatami. The arrangement of rooms was exactly the same as at Takako's place, though the building there was wooden whereas this was ferroconcrete. But the two apartments had something more than that in common. I wondered what it could be.

Looking round me again after sitting down, I realized what it was. There were very few ornaments for a woman's place. Another striking thing was the absence of a single woman's magazine, or of any other kind of weekly.

"What do you do with yourself every day?"

"I'm home most of the time. I go out shopping sometimes, of course. . . ."

She smiled faintly. I knew what the smile meant: it was in a large food store that we'd first struck up an acquaintance.

"I know, I know. I mean, what do you do when you're at home? Read or something?"

"No, just roll about the place."

"Roll about?"

"Mm. Like I had no arms or legs at all."

"What *do* you have, then?"

"I wonder, now. . . ." She chuckled.

"Just a big heart rolling around, eh?" I said.

In fact, there'd been something erotic about her chuckle. It wouldn't have seemed out of place, for instance, if I'd said, "Just a big cunt . . ." It was that kind of atmosphere. Not that I'd said "heart" simply to avoid being crude, though; nor had I intended her to substitute any other word for it. I couldn't say exactly why, but the word "heart" had come out naturally, without anything complicated in the background.

Natsue, however, refused to give up the subject.

"I just stay indoors, blowing up my balloon."

"Balloon? You mean, your—"

"No, no particular part of my body. A pale mauve balloon— you know what I mean?"

I kind of got it. Anyway, the message of the conversation was clearly erotic. Natsue's eyes had gone misty, and her lips were slightly parted. I could tell that her breathing was getting faster as she got up and opened the wooden door into the next room.

It was a Western-style bedroom, with most of the space occupied by a large double bed. She pulled back the cover to reveal a dazzling white expanse of starched sheet. The bed had a wooden frame. Perhaps because the sheets themselves were so fresh, it was the frame that I was aware of. I felt somehow that if you could see inside, it would be soft and syrupy from all the animal essences it had absorbed.

A gray telephone stood on the bedside table.

"Let's go out, after all," I said, momentarily unnerved.

"It's the bed that bothers you, isn't it?"

I muttered something vague; she was right first time, but I couldn't bring myself to admit it.

"You're fussy about the funniest things, aren't you?" she said. I grinned ruefully. "And there was I, expecting it to excite you!"

Just then the phone rang. Natsue put the receiver to her ear, and seemed for a while to be listening to the caller. Then she said,

"Of course—don't you think I'm a good girl?" And she grabbed my wrist, drew it toward her and entwined her own fingers in mine. I could tell from what she'd said that the call was from Hokkaido. She went on speaking in the same position, giving my fingers a tight little squeeze from time to time.

Just as she was saying "Is it snowing up there?" or something equally trivial, I slipped my other hand beneath her sweater. She wasn't wearing a bra, and my fingers made direct contact with her breasts. She wriggled slightly. Not to avoid my fingers, though, but as a sign that she was getting worked up. Even so, the tone of her voice didn't change, and since I didn't want it to, I kept the movements of my fingers under strict control.

Before long, her hand replaced the receiver, but continued to grasp it. In the same position as while she'd been phoning, I slowly slid my fingers off her breast and down her flank. I could feel her skin growing faintly damp with sweat.

Then I noticed that her fingers, which still gripped the receiver as though to hold it down, had tightened, and my feelings got the better of me.

With her slender body clasped in my arms, we fell onto the great bed. Once we'd actually got there, the wooden bed provided a constant spur to my senses.

Thin films of sweat touched and mingled on our two bodies. . . .

Eventually, the bodies separated and I found myself pressed up against Natsue with one hand on her breast as she lay, still naked, facing the ceiling.

"It'd be awkward if you got pregnant now, wouldn't it?"

"Awkward? Yes, very awkward. But I wouldn't mind."

"Why not?"

"Well, because I'd have to go to the doctor, wouldn't I? I love starting a kid and getting him to drag it out again."

Natsue's head had turned to face me, with her nose pressed against my chest, so all I could see was a pink-flushed ear. I gazed at the ear for a while in silence. I'd never met a woman who said that kind of thing before. She always objected to my using a contraceptive, or ejaculating outside her. And since I didn't care for those methods either, I always went along with her wishes.

I suppose it's only natural for people, both men and women, to want to get as much strong, direct pleasure as possible out of sex. For the six years between my wife's death and meeting up with Takako (and occasionally even afterward), I'd relied on prostitutes to satisfy my sexual needs. Most whores don't like stripping off completely. In such cases I would never force things. I'd wait till

67

I was on the job, then start removing the remaining garments. I've never known a woman to object at that stage. Invariably she would go all limp and let my hands do as they pleased. Sometimes she'd actually cooperate, with unobtrusive movements of her shoulders and arms.

It took a great deal of time, they say, before human beings stopped having sex solely for the sake of reproduction. Even now, if you ask me, it's still true to say that where men have *sex* organs, women have *reproductive* organs. No doubt women get a deeper pleasure out of the sex act, but the pleasure is only incidental to the real goal, which is conception.

"That's why," I said to myself, reflecting on what Natsue had just said. Her defiant show of not caring probably stemmed from her very awareness of that fact. But that wasn't all. I started talking, hoping to find out for sure. We were to exchange several times as much conversation that day as we normally did.

"Getting him to drag it out. . . . That's a pretty strange taste. Does it make you feel like some kind of tragic heroine?"

"Don't—"

She started to deny it, then stopped and said,

"But there may be a touch of that, too."

"Masochism?" I asked, continuing the interrogation.

"Who knows?"

"How do you feel when you hear you're pregnant?"

"Not at all bad. I don't feel it's awkward till later."

"I imagine the first reaction's the instinctive one."

"I expect so."

"Then why do you say you enjoy abortions? There must be a touch of masochism there, surely?"

"Yes, it does look like it, doesn't it?"

"Or was it just so much talk?"

"Who knows?"

"If it wasn't awkward to have a kid, would you want one?"

"No, not even then."

The reply wasn't the kind to be taken at face value, so I omitted to ask why and went on:

"If you got pregnant now, could you tell whose kid it was?"

"No."

"Some people say you can tell. . . ."

For the first time, her reply wasn't noncommittal. With the utmost conviction she said,

"Well, they're wrong! There's no way to tell."

The ear visible just in front of my eye was the same rosy pink as ever.

17

An unexpected visitor: Toru Tsunoki.

The look he gave Yumiko as she came in with the tea reminded me of the old Tsunoki. A keen, appraising look, followed by an expression that told me she'd passed the test.

Even now, I felt sure, Tsunoki would have wasted no time making advances to her. In that respect he hadn't changed. This wasn't a moral judgment, mark you: he just happened to be that kind of man. Of course, I admit that somewhere in the back of my mind the business with my wife was mixed up in it too.

"I'm afraid Uda's been bothering you," Tsunoki began in a formal tone. "But there was no suggestion of someone else writing the stuff for you. All I meant was that it was the kind of subject anyone could write about."

His tone seemed to suggest that Uda had been discourteous not only to me but to Tsunoki himself.

"You mean Maki, I suppose?" I said.

"Well, yes. An interesting case, isn't it? I think a day-by-day account would be really worth having."

" 'Interesting'? Yes, I suppose so. . . ."

"I know how you feel, old boy. I must say, though, you ought to look more closely before you leap. I mean, to make sure what you're dealing with." He seemed to have got hold of the wrong end of the stick. But he went on,

"Those people live in a completely different dimension from the likes of us. You'll get nowhere. It's impossible. Though that, of course, is precisely what makes it so interesting. . . ."

His view was the same as Maki's. But he was wrong: it wasn't impossible. The confident assertion only betrayed something of his attitude toward me.

Tsunoki's talking down to you, I told myself.

I had an urge to needle him just as I had Maki.

"Is it so impossible, though?" I said.

"What—you mean you managed it?"

"No, no," I lied. "Maki and I are just friends."

"I bet you tried though, didn't you? Otherwise there wouldn't be anything interesting about the affair."

"What I mean is, I don't believe people like Maki live in a different dimension."

I'd decided to try a different approach to the business. Maki meant nothing much to me: she'd made too little impression physically. What I was more interested in was Maki's past relationships with men, and the lesbianism which had been (or so I was convinced in Maki's case) an outcome of those relationships.

"You don't like feeling you've been made odd man out, eh?"

I felt a stab of hatred for him. But I recovered my cool almost immediately and said,

"You're determined to see things you own way, aren't you? Anyhow, assuming for the moment you're right, who would you say is the other woman?"

"Someone else you know—Tae, of course."

"Tae? . . . She was the pale, pudgy one, wasn't she? With eyes that look as though they're not properly focused."

"That's right. Tae's the woman and Maki the man."

Tsunoki spoke with conviction, and I stayed silent. It was partly, though, because of a sudden urge I'd just had. An urge to try and seduce Tae. . . .

"Suddenly, you see," Tsunoki went on, "a man from an entirely different world bursts in on these two women and turns them upside down. . . . It means you have to play the outsider, but there'd be no interest otherwise. Of course"—his tone turning soothing—"I'm referring to your fictional diary. How about it? You'll do it, won't you? It seems to me you could use this as a way of writing about lesbianism. I'm not asking you to write about yourself."

"I know."

"Not interested?"

"It's not that, but I'd like time to think about it."

"If you've got something else that looks interesting, that'll do as well."

Natsue popped into my mind at that point. But gazing at Tsunoki's lips, which were an unusually vivid red for someone of his age (they were one other thing that hadn't changed), I told another lie.

"No, nothing else. Let me think about it just the same."

18

I had to go away on private business, to the San'in district.

Generally speaking I find traveling just too much bother. When I realized that this time the business in hand definitely required my presence, I spoke about it to Yumiko.

"How'd you like to come along?" I said—mainly, I suppose, to relieve the sense of boredom. You could hardly have called it a serious invitation.

It was only when I saw her expression go tense that I realized the implications of what I'd said. Careless of me. I was about to take it back when she said,

"I've been meaning to tell you for some time—I'm thinking of getting married."

"*That* wasn't what I had in mind when I asked you to come," I said, and added immediately, "All the same, who'd have thought you'd take it into your head to . . .?"

"I know, but . . ."

A faint flush tinged her face and disappeared again.

"Why not, though? It's a woman's vocation, after all."

As I spoke, my mind was running over the events that first brought her to my place as a daily help. In January the previous year, she'd called at my house as a reporter for a woman's magazine. With her slight build and small features, she struck me at once as an attractive girl. But the mild surprise I felt at her appearance was capped the next moment by something more startling. Her lips— she was lightly made up so as to show off her skin to advantage, and the small mouth was painted in with a pale-colored lipstick—parted, and out came the words,

"I've come to ask your views on masturbation."

No sign of embarrassment at all. I thought perhaps I'd misheard, but I hadn't. More words followed, equally unabashed, from those same small lips.

I wondered if she might be too much of a child still for the questions to have any real meaning for her. I took a closer look at the pale face.

"Hold it!—" I said. "How old are you?"

She was young, that was certain, but she was no teen-ager. She might have passed for twenty, but I for one wasn't take in.

"Twenty-three?" I ventured.

A subtle shadow passed over Yumiko's face, and it turned into the face of a woman of twenty-three.

"D'you go around asking questions like that every day?"

"Yes, I do."

"Been doing this work for long?"

"No. I used to be on a film magazine."

"And you had to quit?"

I'd spoken half to myself, but the question seemed to make her shrink. Another girl who's had trouble with men, I thought. My gaze went to the slender neck, and unexpectedly I felt sorry for her.

"You've had enough of this nonsense," I found myself saying. "How'd it be if you came here and helped with the work about the house? It's mostly odd jobs, I'm afraid, but . . ."

To say I felt sorry for her wouldn't really be accurate. There was a touch of a warmer emotion, too. So you could hardly blame her if she took my words as a declaration of interest. In fact, as I watched her nod acquiescence I almost felt as though I'd proposed and been accepted.

In practice, though, my behavior toward her from the next day on, when she started coming, was correctness itself. Why? Because, I suppose, I'd had a bellyful of living with women already. . . .

Fourteen months went by.

It was pleasant to have an attractive young woman around the house, but I was careful not to let the feeling show. As far as I was concerned, my relationship with Yumiko consisted of nothing more than a daily round of small, practical matters. Now, though, she'd suddenly announced her intention of getting married. Could it mean that she'd been waiting to find out my intentions and that she'd officially got tired of doing so? (After all, there's nothing particularly odd these days in a marriage between a man of forty-three and a girl of twenty-four.) I was seized with distaste even before I'd checked whether I was right or not. She stood there, waiting, a black pit yawning in front of me.

"You'd be better off married," I stated flatly. "I'm sure you'd be happier that way."

So it was Maki I invited to accompany me, and she accepted at once. To me Maki looked a safer type of woman. I gave her the ticket for the seat next to mine, and we agreed to meet on the train.

On the afternoon of the appointed day, I'd not been long in my seat when Maki appeared and took her place next to me on the window side. No sooner was she seated than she pressed her face to the glass and said, looking out, "It's a lovely day."

The scene beyond the window was shining in the sunlight. After a while, she settled herself back in her seat and asked, unexpectedly, "D'you remember the way I imagined you at first?"

"I certainly do, it was so wide of the mark. I had a wife who was unfaithful to me but though I knew about it I went on living with her without complaining. Or something along those lines."

"Talking of wives, though—I hear you're not married. I didn't know till recently. So this is just like a honeymoon, isn't it?" She laughed, and in a different tone of voice went on, "If I really felt like that, you'd be shocked, wouldn't you?"

She was quite right. I felt a touch of shame, in fact, at the way my reflexes had braced me against attack. In reality, her being able to poke fun at me made me feel all the safer. Why, then, should it produce such an automatic emotional reaction in me?

I was still wondering when she went on,

"You've often said I ought to dig back into my past a bit. But I get the feeling that *you* ought to, too."

Previously, when I myself had said something similar to her, my words had turned on me, and Keiko's face had risen up in front of my eyes. I'd sworn that I wasn't going back into the past any more —that there was no need to—and I'd shaken my head to dispel the image.

This time, though, I nodded without fighting against what Maki said. Taken by itself, the business with Keiko had begun to seem rather a feeble reason for doing so.

"So now we're off together in search of the answer, are we? Your answer, and my answer. . . ."

Shortly after that, the bell signaling our departure started to ring. It was as though the train were setting off into the darkness of the past. . . .

19

We stayed two nights in the small town that was our destination. I took two rooms at the hotel, and we slept independently of each other. Much of the time I was out on business, leaving Maki alone in the hotel.

I finally cleared up my work by dinnertime on the evening of the third day. Alone with Maki at dinner I got a bit drunk, savoring my release from the irksome practical affairs of the past days.

"It's a long time since I last saw the sun rise," I said.

"Then let's leave by the early train tomorrow morning," suggested Maki, in a practical mood.

"When you put it like that, I can't be bothered. I was thinking of getting up late tomorrow and taking the afternoon train to Kyoto. Then we could stay overnight if we felt like it."

"That's all very well—," said Maki with a disconsolate expression.

"Are *you* so set on seeing the sun rise, then?"

"I like riding a train as it speeds through the early morning air—how does that satisfy you?" she said; and with some asperity: "You know, I think you're very insensitive. You say we could stay in Kyoto—d'you mean in separate rooms again?"

I'm quite aware that in some ways I'm thoughtless, but I still failed to grasp what Maki was getting at.

"How am I supposed to take that?"

"Well, anybody'd think you didn't see me as a woman at all."

"You don't mean that seriously, surely?"

I spoke calmly enough, but I sensed that Maki wasn't quite as safe as I'd thought. At the same time, I had to admit that this was only to be expected; after all, hadn't I myself denied that she lived in a "different dimension"?

"Yes . . . maybe it was just a slip of the tongue."

"I thought we agreed the other day we'd just be friends."

"It was you who said that. Did I give any answer?"

"Not that I can remember, actually. Anyway, we'd better go to sleep early tonight."

"I warn you, I'll only wake up earlier tomorrow morning," she said sulkily.

"In that case," not to be outdone, "we can catch the early morning train. All right?"

20

We took the seven-thirty train. The day was fine and smelled of morning. At eight o'clock, a young ticket inspector came hurrying into our car. The cabin reserved for the conductor was directly behind my seat, and I could hear the two men standing there talking. The inspector was reporting that he'd found two passengers without tickets in the next car. A boy of about five and a girl of about four.

I wondered if I'd misheard. But the small boy the inspector had with him when he came back about five minutes later reached no further than the tall young man's waist. The girl was shorter still.

"Excuse me," I said, addressing the conductor, who looked about my own age, "but those kids look scared. Why don't you sit them down here?" I pointed to the vacant seats facing ours. "If you take them into your cabin, they'll probably feel worse."

"Good idea," the man said, quick on the uptake. "I expect it was the passengers in the next car that frightened them with all their questions. Not that you can blame them for being curious. Even *I've* never come across a case like this."

I grinned to myself. He'd successfully forestalled any desire on my part either to question or show curiosity.

I surveyed the young pair, now seated directly in front of us. The boy had a screwdriver and a gimlet clasped in his right hand.

"And what are you going to do with *those*?" I'd asked the question before I could stop myself.

The boy seemed to know what I meant from the gaze fixed on his right hand.

"I've got to find a job," he replied in a tense little voice. I looked puzzled.

"They say they're going to Osaka," the conductor explained. "But whereabouts in Osaka I've no idea. No idea what station he and his sister got on at, either."

"Sister? . . ." I began, and went no further. Their features weren't alike, and it hadn't even occurred to me to see them as brother and sister.

"Here, sonny—who's your little friend?" asked Maki, getting the point at once.

"This . . . this is Kakko," was all the answer.

Maki asked no more questions, but took a can of candy out of her suitcase and tilted it over each of the children's hands in turn. There was a dry sound of hard objects in contact with metal, and fruit drops rolled into the open palms.

Almost immediately the kids began to lose their frightened look, and the girl's attention turned to the scenery rushing past the window. Before long, her small nose was glued to the glass.

It was then that I noticed the faint smell. What was it, though? Something stirred inside me, but refused to come to the surface. I went on wondering. For a while my mind dragged its feet unwillingly, then I suddenly realized: it was the smell of community life.

I couldn't be sure, though. Perhaps the idea was suggested by memories of the smell of life in the army. But even assuming there was anything corresponding to army life nowadays, the children were obviously too young to have any connection with it.

Could it be the smell of some public institution, then? They didn't seem to have any physical disabilities, so perhaps they'd run away from an orphanage.

I was looking at the boy and girl, mentally comparing them, when something caught my eye: the thermos, enameled in a cheerful flower pattern, that sat on the seat between them. It wasn't the portable type, but the kind you set on the table, with a solid, stable shape. I could imagine it standing on a big table of rough wood. And I could see the orphans, lots of them, seated around the table. . . .

The door to our car opened, and a pair of young women came in with a large box slung between them: the girls who sold food and drink on the train.

The moment they began to cry their wares, the little girl, who'd been watching the scenery with her nose pressed to the window, turned round in a hurry and said in a small voice,

"Oh, ice cream!"

"Buy them some," I said to Maki, "and some orange juice to go with it."

The girl clutched at her ice cream cup. Simultaneously, the fruit drop was ejected through her small lips.

"Personally," said the conductor, "I'd let them go on to Osaka, but . . ."

"Even so, it'd probably be better to send them back where they came from," I said, and realized that I'd already made up my mind that they were runaways from an orphanage.

"That's all very well," the man said, looking dubious, "but I don't *know* where they came from."

"Nor do I, but the smell . . ."

I looked at the two children absorbed in their ice cream, then my hand went out to the thermos, grasped it, and raised it so that I could peer at the bottom. I don't know what made me do it: "sixth sense," I suppose.

"Here—," I exclaimed. The metal base of the flask had writing on it.

"Found something, sir?" said the conductor, peering closer. I showed him the inscription: "Presented by Kazamura."

Kazamura, no doubt, was the man who'd donated the thermos. So it looked as though the smell was the smell of an institution, as I'd thought. In a low voice I gave the conductor a summary of my deductions.

"I see." With his eyes on my face he raised his left wrist to the level of his chin, then shifted his gaze to his watch.

"We're stopping in seven minutes. Either way, we'd better put them off at the next station and have them checked up on. I'll telephone ahead to let people know, if you'll keep them here till the next stop."

He disappeared into his cabin.

Before long the train halted. It was an unexpectedly small station for an express stop, and the platform was nearly deserted. I caught sight of two young station officials standing there looking expectant.

The conductor handed the two children over to the young men, and they started walking toward the stairs. A bridge led over the tracks to the platform with the ticket barrier.

One of the officials took the lead and the other, the thermos in his right hand and two half-empty bottles of orange juice in his left, brought up the rear, with the children in between. Maki and I watched the scene from our seats. Clasped in the boy's right hand I could see the screwdriver and gimlet, which the adults, it seemed, hadn't been able to get away from him.

They started up the stairs.

The children didn't turn round. There was nothing for them to look back for. The boy was hidden behind the official's uniform, but I caught sight of the little girl, stretching her legs out almost horizontal with the effort of negotiating each step. She was all in red: red jacket, red shorts—a small red pepper planting each foot laboriously in turn on the next step up. The official made no move to help her. His hands were full; the back of his dark blue uniform climbed slowly and without expression, keeping pace with the children.

Suddenly, the stairs seemed to be leading away into a black nothingness beyond.

"All that effort climbing. . . ." I muttered, and at that moment the train started. The scene beyond the windows changed to an expanse of fields and paddies, but still the children seemed to linger in the empty seats opposite ours.

"Oh, look!" Maki exclaimed suddenly in an unnatural voice. The voice was faint but with an underlying force. It was as though she'd tried so fiercely to repress it that when it finally emerged it was like a wisp of steam rising from her mouth.

"What is it?" I asked. I felt somehow she'd suddenly collapsed against me and I was supporting her. Without speaking, she pointed downward.

A small, mauve lump formed a point of shining wet color on the dusty floor. It was the fruit drop the little girl had let fall from her lips a while ago.

It lay there, summing up in itself the whole little episode. But I was reluctant to fall in with the unnatural tone of Maki's voice, so I said as coolly as possible:

"All right—something about the color of a cheap fruit drop happens to make an impression on you, but so what?"

"Don't be—"

"Well, go on—tell me then: what happened just now?"

"They should never have been born."

"I wonder if anyone has the right to say that? *They*'re not responsible for their birth."

"Nor are their parents."

I looked at her and said nothing.

"But they'll manage somehow, won't they?" she went on as though urging me to nod agreement.

"They usually do."

The little boy seemed to have a mind of his own. It wasn't impossible that in future he'd get on in the world—make a pile of money, even. But then what? The mauve of the fruit drop, all wet with saliva, still came and went obstinately in my mind's eye.

21

Whenever I wanted a woman, I'd call either Takako or Natsue. Usually I was hard put to it to make the choice.

One evening in April, I saw Takako—the first meeting in a month during which I'd been away with Maki and met Natsue any number of times. Not that I hadn't hesitated before picking on Natsue. I'd wavered every time, but in the end it was she I called, and invariably my invitation was accepted.

Not having phoned Takako for so long, I went to meet her with something like a sense of obligation. But the reality was satisfying enough. As usual, she was embarrassed at the start, but her very shyness contrived to suggest desire. Before long, modesty was cast to the winds and she went wild. Her body twisted and half rose off the bed, her thick black hair strayed over the tatami, she gave long, lingering moans in a thin, clear voice unlike any that Natsue ever produced. . . .

Later, when she was dressed again and seated primly in front of me, she said without warning,

"I've a good mind to get married."

Takako sometimes had startling flashes of insight. On one occasion I was in bed with her at a hotel when I suddenly remembered some work that I had to get done before the morning. I'd said nothing to her about it, and I was sure my behavior had given no sign. Even so, the moment our bodies separated she started hurriedly getting dressed without even having a bath.

"What's the hurry?" I'd asked as she was pulling on her stockings.

She turned her face to look at me without straightening up.

"It's you who's in a hurry, isn't it?"

The woman who'd said that might well have sensed the feeling of obligation that motivated me this time. But I suspected it was something more.

"That's rather sudden, isn't it?" I ventured.

"Sudden? I've been waiting for years, haven't I?"

"There's no point in waiting. I thought you knew that from the start."

"No point, I know. I've realized it myself. That's the kind of man you are, isn't it?"

"The kind of man . . . ?" adding, to make sure, "You mean, I'm not the kind to leave his wife and kids for . . ." But she just watched me without saying anything.

"I've never once seen your face properly," she went on, with no sense, I'm sure, of changing the subject. "Always the area of your chin." Either way, she almost certainly didn't believe I had a wife and kids. "I was twenty-four when I met you, and I'll soon be thirty."

"Nearly two years to go, surely?"

"Two years is nothing. People get funny ideas about a girl who's still single at thirty."

"What people?"

"Ordinary people. The people round about, of course. . . . Isn't it the same with you?"

Her words made it quite clear that she didn't think I was married. But I'd no inclination to set the record straight from my side. I was more interested in other things.

82

"You've taken a fancy to someone, I suppose?"

"Don't be silly. . . . I've had any number of proposals over the last four years. I refused the lot, but maybe it's about time now."

"Mightn't be a bad idea. Though I suspect you've already made up your mind anyway."

"Not exactly, but . . ."

"Have you been to bed?"

I felt a stir of something like jealousy. Something hurt slightly inside me at the idea of another man witnessing all the subtle little responses of her body.

"To bed?"

"With him—with the other man."

"Oh, come on! Was I any different from usual just now?"

"You were, in fact. More passionate. Stimulated by a sense of guilt." I made it sound like a joke.

So far, Takako had always contrived to suggest I was the only man in her life. But I didn't trust her. I couldn't believe she hadn't been to bed with any other man for the past four years. When she got excited her lips, which were small and normally shaped at ordinary times, seemed to curl outward. I hated the idea of another man seeing them like that. But along with the repugnance went another feeling, a suspicion that it would be a load off my own back. It took me by surprise. Maybe the reason why I hadn't seen her during the past month was that she was beginning to be a burden. Yet I hadn't detected any signs that way in myself.

"When will you get married, assuming you do?"

"The sooner the better, I feel. Before I start having second thoughts."

"We'd better not meet any more once you're married, had we?"

I wasn't without my regrets. But Takako said in a matter-of-fact tone,

"I don't think so."

She dwindled perceptibly in my mind, till she was no bigger than a pea.

"The odd phone call wouldn't matter, would it?"

Already I could say it without any particular regret. But she made no reply, so I went on:

"Does he work for a living?"

"Yes."

"Will you have a wedding?"

"It's the usual thing, isn't it?"

"Well then, I'll give you a call sometime after you get back from your honeymoon."

I succeeded in making her promise to call me in a few days and let me know the date of the wedding and her new telephone number.

22

I saw Natsue the evening of the day Takako got married. Natsue knew nothing of Takako's existence.

I'd noticed recently that Natsue and I were talking more. At one time, the regular routine had been for us to take a room at an inn, strip off, converse for a while in sounds that were not speech, then have a bath and go our respective ways without further ado. My relationship with Takako had been much the same (it was I who determined the pattern, the women just went along with it). I'm sure that had a lot to do with Takako's remark that she'd never seen my face properly.

That evening, Natsue and I talked together a good deal.

"Do you have any urge to get married?"

I hadn't concealed from Natsue that I lived by myself.

"None at all. A man only has to suggest we live together and I take an instant dislike to him."

"Feeling resentful, eh? I guess some man did the dirty on you."

"Maybe, once. But it's different now. Nowadays the one thing I'm interested in is physical pleasure. Marriage means living for completely different things. You have to fit in with what *society* wants."

"I see."

Just about this time, Takako would be sitting next to the man on the train. I began to feel I understood something of what she was up to.

"Very interesting," I went on. "But don't you think your approach is a bit wide and shallow for someone living for the senses?"

"I wonder."

Her voice as she looked me full in the face was low and a little husky. It didn't really match her slender body, but it went well with the large, moist eyes and the lips that were always slightly parted.

"Haven't you noticed?" she said.

"Noticed what?"

"Ever since we got to know each other, I've always come to meet you whenever you asked me, haven't I? There were several times when it was awkward, of course. . . ."

"Yes . . . I suppose you're right."

The fact struck me as though for the first time. I was mulling it over when she added,

"I'm thinking of moving."

"Moving?"

"Yes. How about it?"

"Mightn't be a bad idea," I stalled. I wasn't quite sure what the idea was. She might mean she was leaving her rich lover. But that would be a bore. My feelings remained unclear, even to myself.

23

One afternoon a week later I called Takako at her new home. I heard the receiver being lifted and a voice reply,

"Hello? Mrs. Moriya speaking."

The voice was Takako's, but the surname was new to me. The voice sounded relaxed, the voice of a woman no longer afraid of what people said behind her back.

"Takako?" I said to make sure.

"Oh, hello!" I sensed a touch of embarrassment.

"You sound quite settled in," I said.

"Actually I'm bored to tears."

"I doubt it somehow. . . . Anyway—you can tell me now, can't you?"

"Tell you what?"

"How many men you've been involved with in the last four years. Three?"

"What makes you say three?" The voice had turned noncommittal, a reaction that could well mean I'd hit on the right figure.

"There *were* others, weren't there?"

"Only one. . . ."

"Once, two or three months ago—remember?—you wouldn't see me because you said you had a cold. He was there then, wasn't he? How many times did you sleep with him—ten, say?"

"Around four. . . ."

"Is it the same man you've married?"

"No, someone else."

"Why didn't you marry that one?"

"Why? I suppose we just weren't right for each other."

However long you live, it's impossible to turn your back on society completely. The marriage system, though, can be ignored indefinitely. That, more or less, was what Takako had done; or so I'd thought, but I'd been wrong.

I didn't believe her when she said "only one," but even if there only had been one, it meant she'd played with him for a stake. It wouldn't have bothered me if she'd simply decided at some stage to give him her body. That part of it didn't worry me. What rankled was the underhand scheming involved in a woman's putting up her naked body in a calculated move to secure marriage.

But in a way I understood. I liked Takako, both mentally and physically. I'd almost never felt distaste at anything that went on in her mind. The only unpleasantness I felt, in fact, was now. . . .

Quite suddenly, I began to be excited by the mental picture of Takako, after her initial coyness, spreading her thighs wide open for another man. The man himself was blank save for the vaguest of outlines, which made the scene all the more vivid.

"Let's hear your voice," I said into the receiver.

"Voice?"

"You know what I mean. I want to hear that voice just once more."

"Not if you ask in *that* tone," she said and the receiver was silent. After a while, a sound came as though she was having difficulty controlling her breathing, then she suddenly said,

"That's enough." Her voice was collected. "You know how I like to keep a place tidy, don't you?"

"Yes, now you say so. Not that I know what kind of room you're in now."

"I'm sitting on the sofa holding the phone, with my feet up. There's a vase on the side table, with a whole mass of poppies stuck in it. A little while ago they suddenly scattered, and the floor's covered all over with deep orange petals and little black bits."

"I can see it very clearly."

"It looks terribly obscene." She seemed to be having trouble with her breathing again. "So please . . . won't you ring off now?"

In my mind's eye I had a vision of Takako beneath another man: abandoned, crying out loud. "This woman has got *married*," I told myself, and rejecting the mental picture resumed in a more normal voice,

"Right, let's stop this. I'd better not call you any more."

Without waiting, I slowly replaced the receiver. As I did so, I could clearly sense this woman with whom I'd been intimate for four years turning into a stranger. It was some little while before the idea stopped feeling odd.

24

I remember a character in a foreign novel I read when I was at high school—a young gangster whose front teeth, top and bottom, had all broken off and been replaced with gold. Here and there, his body was pocked with small holes, the scars left by bullets. The kisses of his golden mouth were cold, and the fingertips of the women who held his body would slip into the holes in his back. In the story, a married woman of good family becomes hopelessly obsessed with him physically. . . . I felt at the time that I could understand her feelings pretty well. But around the same time, I was surprised to learn that a friend's elder sister—a good-looking girl—collected reproductions of paintings of nude women.

"I think a woman's body is the most beautiful thing in the world," the sister had said.

But now, twenty-odd years later, I could dimly appreciate how she felt. When two attractive women embrace, they exist in a purely sensual world. No pregnancy, no domesticity, just the play of the senses. A woman is far closer acquainted than a man with the subtleties of the female body. A woman can bring another woman's body to fever pitch in much the same way as her own. The two bodies with their swelling breasts touch each other not as ivy embraces the tree but as ivy entwining with ivy—searching out each other, the long hair tangling, till everything, finally, melts into one. Into a pale pink liquid afloat in a purple gas—or perhaps, a deep red solid. . . .

In theory, it could be a beautiful sight.

But what about the lesbianism that people make such a fuss about these days?

A couple of women hold a wedding ceremony, and the weeklies go to town. What vulgar nonsense, though. . . . One of them usually wears men's clothes, and is short and thickset. "In the lesbian world," I read once, "the woman who plays the male role is called 'butch' and the female 'femme.' Miss X uses male speech, so naturally she's butch. Her hair is drawn tightly back, she wears glasses with thick brown frames, and dresses in dark blue suits . . . just like the typical white-collar worker." This kind of woman strikes me as wretched and pathetic. I immediately suspect there's something wrong that she can't tell people about.

About a month after I got home from my trip, I met Maki. Since she was a pleasant girl, it seemed natural to me to meet her for a talk whenever I had time to spare. But I had no positive urge to sleep with her.

"You're a cold fish!" she started the moment she saw me.

"You shouldn't say that, surely? People will suspect your lesbianism isn't genuine."

"D'you really think so?"

"If you don't see it, then something's seriously wrong. Tell me, though—why do some lesbians like dressing up as men? Surely it's a kind of penis envy?"

"None of the girls *I* know wears men's clothes," she began, as though she belonged to some tribe apart. "But according to one of them, penises have nothing to do with it, since they can never get physical satisfaction with a man anyway."

"Which proves, doesn't it, that you and your pals *talk* about penises."

"The subject came up because someone read something similar

89

to what you've just said. Some of the others said they tried to forget about penises as much as possible."

"It seems there are lesbians and lesbians. . . . All the same, I can't help feeling sorry for women who get no physical satisfaction in bed with a man," I said, and told her about an old Hitchcock movie I'd seen on TV a few days earlier. The subject wasn't so irrelevant as it might seem.

"I've a high regard for Hitchcock as an entertainer," I said, "so I was looking forward to it at first. But it was a downright bore. All about a woman who got married but had an absolute dread of going to bed with her husband. The reason was that subconsciously she was suffering the effects of some childhood trauma connected with men. I'm not sure what made it so dull—the hackneyed Freudian analysis or the simple illogicality in the fact that she needn't have got married at all if she hated it so much. Probably a bit of both. I wonder, though, why the psychoanalytical approach immediately dries up my interest? Even though, of course, it's usually on the mark. . . . Perhaps it all seems a bit too pat for me."

"What you're hinting at, I suppose," said Maki, her eyes hard, "is that all lesbians are like that because of some trauma associated with men."

"Not *all* of them, but . . ."

"But me, you mean."

"You *did* say it made you sick, you know." And for the first time I took a searching look at her face. My immediate impression on meeting her for the first time in a month had been that she'd changed; now I found that she'd shaved her eyebrows and penciled in new ones, and was using a pale shade of lipstick.

"Yes, of course," I thought to myself almost automatically.

"What's wrong? Why're you looking at me like that?"

"I was thinking that somehow you're getting the real look."

"Real look? . . ." She smiled briefly, then her expression changed to a mixture of shame and anger.

She'd said that she hadn't felt sick when she had sex with me. But the next time I'd taken her to a hotel I'd left her alone. Mightn't that have been what prompted her to give up men once and for all? Watching her face as I wondered, I began to feel it had been changed by something more than a different style of makeup.

"Is it Tae?" I ventured.

"Is *what* Tae?"

"The other woman. Tsunoki told me that she was the woman and you the man."

"It's all wrong from the start to think in terms of 'male' and 'female' roles. All it means is that the one who's made advances to takes the passive role."

"That might apply the first time round, but . . . Myself, I'd have said you were the feminine kind."

I remembered the smell of scent on her body.

"There you go again! Tae's just an ordinary girl. She doesn't play around. Not that *that* makes you safe—she got syphilis a while ago. The boy she's been going steady with was unfaithful to her and came back with a dose."

"I can hardly imagine Tae with syphilis."

"The doctor got a shock, too. I was scared myself, so I had a checkup."

"What was there for you to get scared about? Ah—so Tae *was* . . ."

"No! Because of that business with you."

I grinned ruefully. But my suspicion about the relationship between Maki and Tae still lingered.

"And what was the result of the checkup?"

"Negative."

"Which means there was nothing between you and Tae?"

"Oh, stop being so suspicious!"

"But you were suspicious of me too, weren't you?"

"I've good reason, haven't I?"

"What about you, then?—there must be someone else, or nothing would make sense. It's only natural to be suspicious, surely?"

"There is someone. But it's not Tae. I just want to keep the record straight."

"Who is it, then?"

"I can't tell you."

"So you're clamming up?"

"That's right."

"You said just now that none of your friends dressed up as men —you're sure that's the truth?"

"Of course it is. I don't go for such obvious . . ."

"You prefer the subtle play of the senses, eh?"

"Yes. Yes, that's right."

She spoke as though it should be perfectly obvious, but my understanding of the world of lesbianism was still inadequate. Or rather, was still full of prejudices.

There was a lingering furtiveness in Maki's face that evening, like the silvery trail left by a slug. It made me want to question her, and I asked all kinds of things about female homosexuality.

"You can't expect me to answer all that at once," she said. "I'll put the answers down in writing sometime soon and leave them at 'Loco' with Yuzuru."

We were talking in a small restaurant away from the center of town. As soon as we'd finished eating and drunk our coffee, we left and went our separate ways.

25

I'm fond of looking at pictures. Whenever I travel, I pass up the famous tourist spots but visit the art galleries. Late one afternoon about half a month later, I found myself at a loose end, so I started looking through a collection of reproductions. I toyed with a volume of Van Gogh, then went on to Gauguin. Both of them impressed me, but in the Gauguin collection my attention was particularly drawn to the well-known painting *Whence Come We? Who Are We? Where Are We Going?* The picture, which is said to have borrowed techniques from the Japanese woodblock print, is somehow flat and murky, with little contrast of light and shadow, and a hint of death in the air. That and the title combined to have a powerful effect on me.

We live to learn that all is vain—the words sprang to mind unbidden.

One passage in the note to the picture said, "Is the picture, then, a reply to the three questions? No—it is the questions themselves. The examination of these three questions is what constitutes human life." Which resembled the quotation I'd just recalled. And yet, somehow, it was very different.

Whence Come We? . . . Personally, I knew nothing of my own family tree beyond my great-grandfather, but within those limits, at least, there were no suicides, murderers, or madmen. Suddenly, I found myself wondering what might turn up if one traced the line back further. The family line disappeared into the darkness a short way in front of my eyes, but if I were to plunge ahead regardless, what extraordinary characters might not loom up out of that darkness? Was it really true that if you pressed on indefinitely you came up against a bunch of monkeys? If so, what *kind* of monkeys? . . .

I decided to go out for a drink.

As I took my seat at the bar in "Loco," Yuzuru the bartender held out a white envelope and said in his usual effeminate voice,

"Maki left this for you about five days ago."

It was sealed. I tore it open and took out the contents. Four sheets of lined paper.

I set about reading it there and then as I drank my whisky.

   – Does loving a person of the other sex really represent maturity in a human being? Is it normal to be able to love only

93

one sex, or isn't it, rather, abnormal? The question is one we women are always asking ourselves.

— Almost all of us manage our lives perfectly efficiently, both as individuals and in relation to society. To look on homosexuality as a kind of morbid symptom or to talk of a "cure" is an insult to us. Admittedly, many of us would like to escape from the anxiety and loneliness that comes from constituting a society apart. But most find that this desire only heightens the sense of isolation and estrangement, and we end up by returning to the place where we feel most content and most at ease.

— Even we, of course, do have a certain hankering after men, but the unconscious desire not to get caught is so strong that love gets changed into something different, and the sex too is less satisfying than with the same sex. Some people believe it's impossible to feel any definite love for a man if physical satisfaction is not possible. Of course, repeated contact with a man gives rise in time to affection and in some cases to a lasting relationship. But for the woman concerned the man occupies at most twenty per cent of her feelings; the relationship may serve socially as a camouflage, but that is all: she remains a homosexual and not a bisexual.

— In many cases an overbearing father has created an aversion to men. Quite a number, too, have had the experience of being ignored or rejected by their fathers in the early years when a father's love is most essential. Some people (not you, Mr. Nakata) believe that too much clinging to the father leads to anxiety about incest and a withdrawal from relationships with the opposite sex, but I very much doubt it, since in such a situation there'd be a strong, reflex impulse to look for a father substitute.

— Where some emotional or physical hurt is incurred during that period, it seems more likely that the woman would continue to long for the ideal man of her imagination while rejecting male sexuality, and would turn to her own sex to heal the wound. There are some women who have had strong incestuous feelings toward their own mothers, or have actually had homosexual experience with them.

– Miss A was the only daughter of a family secure both socially and economically, but marital relations between her parents were bad, and she still can't get on with her father. As a small child, she often saw her father beating up her mother. Then, when she was twelve or thirteen, she happened to see her father naked and was so shocked that she was sick (shock will produce vomiting in quite a large number of female homosexuals). Even after leaving high school, when she was seduced (half forcibly) by a male, the sight of the male penis made her vomit, and nothing apparently was possible.

Although in places the notes were muddled in their logic, they really got down to the unconscious—which was, of course, the area at which all my questions had been chiefly directed. What attracted my interest apart from this, though, was Maki's attempt to defend herself for seeing me and the element of confession that it revealed. In particular, I suspected that the item about Miss A was to be taken as referring to Maki herself.

"What've you go there—a love letter?" put in Yuzuru as I was reading.

"No, just a note about some business matter."

"Honest? Shall I try calling Maki?"

"Yes, that's an idea," I replied.

"She said to ask you to wait," said Yuzuru as he replaced the receiver and turned back to me. "She'll be right round."

I shoved Maki's notes half-read into my pocket. As I did so, my fingers contacted a box of matches, which I took out to light myself a cigarette.

Idly mulling over what Maki had written, I remembered how many times she'd used the word "we." I began to feel a bit irritated by it: you felt she was deliberately stressing that she lived in a world apart.

I took the sheets of paper out of my pocket again.

This is how the rest went:

— In the end, lesbians who have physical relations with males come to have no feelings at all about sex with them. At first, of course, the absence of any wish to get used to the act with males, and the strong impulse to reject any idea of loving a male, makes them feel a more intense disgust and sense of impurity than an ordinary woman would. Sometimes, too, they feel that the male is violating a place that should be reserved for the expression of love between women. However, if they happen to fall for the male *as a human being* [my italics: Nakata], they quite often find they are able to do things like fellatio.

A lot of things struck me about this particular part.

The word Maki used in opposition to "woman" was not "man," but "male." What lay behind this distinction? Somehow the word "male," deliberately used like that, carried a suggestion of the animal, and of resentment against it. There was something very raw about it.

There were obscure passages, too. I'd have understood, for example, if she'd written "if they happen to fall for a male they quite often find they are able to do things like fellatio"; what made it odd was the intrusion of "as a human being." The effect was almost humorous, but the humor was obviously unintended.

The ambiguity of what she'd written began to irritate me.

Crushing the cigarette out in the ashtray, I lit another without pausing. As I did so, I noticed that the label of the matchbox in my hand was unfamiliar. One side was plain white; the other was light blue, with a picture of two fish on it in white. Two white fish side by side, with wide-open mouths and light blue circles for eyes. They provided a background for the words of a song, superimposed on them in black:

> Tell me, seagull, when's the tide?
> *Hey, ho, over the seas*
> "Pray, sir, ask the waves," she cried,
> *Hey, ho, over the seas*
> "Seagulls ne'er for long may bide."
> *Hey, ho, away we go*

I'd no idea where or when I'd put the matches in my pocket.

All of a sudden my mind relaxed. I began sorting out various things I remembered about Maki.

I'd asked her to travel with me because I thought she was harmless as far as I was concerned. Though I hadn't yet realized then that she had such a definite place in a different world from mine, her attitude to relations between men and women was reassuringly negative. During our trip, a few cracks had developed in that attitude, but from then on something about her had changed, as though she'd declared full allegiance to the exclusive world of women.

Curiosity about that world had made me question her in detail. Her replies all suggested that she'd belonged there ever since she was born.

But there were odd lapses in the notes she'd written, particularly in the last part. I realized that it was the discrepancy between that fact and her constant use of the pronoun "we" that got on my nerves.

Judging from fragmentary remarks and facial expressions, it seemed safe to assume that the cause of her "symptoms" lay in her relations with men. But so far I knew nothing definite about them.

"Does Maki belong here?" I ventured to Yuzuru.

"*Belong* here?"

He gave me a dubious look. I suspected that though Maki came to "Loco" ostensibly as a customer, she got a kickback for it. Otherwise, why had Yuzuru been so quick to get her on the phone?

It was barely dark outside, and there were only two other customers in the bar. In a low voice I told Yuzuru of my suspicion.

"Oh really!" he giggled, covering his mouth with his hand. "Maki's family's well off."

"Maybe, but she doesn't get on well with her father, does she?"

I spoke with the idea of finding out just how far the things Maki had written about so impersonally tallied with her own experience. Of course, I'd no idea how much Yuzuru knew about her affairs.

"Hey, did she tell you about that?" He stared at me suspiciously.

"No, not exactly. . . ."

"Then how come you know about it?"

"Why—shouldn't I?"

"It's not a question of 'shouldn't.' But you don't look the sort people confide their personal troubles to."

"I see. Well, generally I'm not. But it depends on the case."

Without warning Yuzuru dropped his voice.

"Shall I tell you something personal about Maki, then?"

"Are you so well up in her affairs?"

"Not well up, but we're good friends. And I get to hear the gossip."

It was true they seemed friendly enough together—though what two homosexuals, one male and one female, saw in each other was beyond me. Maki, certainly, would have denied outright any suggestion that it was the attraction of fellow sufferers. After all, the notes I'd just read said, "To look on homosexuality as a kind of morbid symptom or to talk of a 'cure' is an insult to us."

At this point Yuzuru dropped his voice still lower and whispered, "I'm sure Maki's a virgin."

Involuntarily, I glanced at his face. Apparently he had the same

98

idea about Maki's and my relationship as Tsunoki. But I kept my expression blank.

"Why?" I prompted.

"I *know*."

"Know what?"

"Why she became a lesbian."

Here was something I wanted to know myself.

"You asked her?"

"Gossip. Reliable gossip."

His account was long-winded and rambling. What it boiled down to was this. She'd fallen in love with a young man. It had taken them a long time to get into bed, and when they finally did so the man was impotent. It turned out he was a fag.

As Yuzuru wound up his story, I seemed to detect a spiteful gleam in his eye. I couldn't tell whether it was directed at Maki or himself. Or perhaps I'd only imagined it in the first place.

If the story was true, it at least provided a concrete explanation of why she felt sick just sitting next to a man. But something still bothered me. What had driven the young man into giving the game away by going to bed with Maki in the first place?

I mentioned this doubt of mine to Yuzuru. Maybe, I suggested, the youngster had thought he might manage it.

"I wouldn't be surprised," said Yuzuru.

"Then he must have *wanted* to be able to make love to a woman?"

"Could be," he said. "It takes all sorts to make a world," he added coolly, this time with a definitely malicious gleam in his eye. Probably directed, I felt, at the young man.

I was remembering how, on that first occasion with Maki, I hadn't done anything to her and she'd said, "What's wrong, can't you make love?" I'd sensed a note of pain in her voice, and thought it odd. Maybe at the time she'd wanted to make love successfully with a man, so as to heal the wound the first experience had inflicted.

99

For a moment, Maki no longer seemed so safe.

But I soon shook off the feeling. In Maki's eyes, a middle-aged man like me would provide a convenient testing ground and nothing more.

I remembered how I'd told Maki that I felt like a piece of litmus paper.

That was already several months ago.

26

The door opened and Maki walked in. Unseen by her, Yuzuru put a finger to his lips and winked, presumably as a warning to me to keep the conversation to myself.

As before, Maki's eyebrows were thin, penciled lines and she wore a pale-colored lipstick. For whose eyes did a woman make herself up, I wondered. Probably it varied from individual to individual, but I'd a feeling that in more cases than not it was for the benefit of other women rather than men or herself. To me, though, the stuff on Maki's face looked less like makeup than the mark of some secret society.

I felt a sense of challenge stirring inside me, a mildly aggressive feeling: if Maki was going to display the mark so conspicuously, then I'd force her to betray her allegiance.

" 'We women,' eh?" I heard myself mutter.

"What are you getting at?" she demanded accusingly, seating herself on the stool next to mine at the bar.

"I just remembered how often the word 'we' crops up in that thing you wrote for me."

"You've just read it, have you?"

"Yes. Quite interesting. . . . A bit too defensive, but—"

"It isn't defensive!"

"What beats me, though, is why you should be willing to go to a hotel with me. Surely it's an act of treachery to 'your' world?"

"What a one-track mind! I thought I wrote it all down for you."

"The thing that interested me most about what you wrote was the way your unconscious shows through. Sometimes you were aware of what you were writing and sometimes you weren't. Judging from that, I'd say that your symptoms . . ."

I used the word deliberately, keeping an eye on Maki's face as I spoke.

"Symptoms?" she demanded, just as I'd expected. "It's nothing to do with symptoms. I thought I explained that in what I wrote."

"That's what muddles things," I said. "I think perhaps you'd do better to agree that they are in fact symptoms. In your case, the source of the disease is men; it's men who got you all dammed up inside."

" 'The source of the disease'? Thanks a lot. Anyway, think what you like for the moment. Just remember, though, that if you dam up a stream you sometimes get a beautiful lake. I've a feeling that in your case you can't see the lake for the dam."

I'd wondered, in fact, about the possible existence of a "lake." What she said wasn't entirely nonsense.

I looked at her. The shut-in impression had got still stronger. No doubt about it, this was a different Maki from the one I'd known before. Even so, the fact remained that the notes she'd written for me were muddled and obscure in places.

I had a little dialogue with myself:

"Getting irritable again?"

"That's overdoing it a bit. Just a little impatient."

"Oh . . . impatient."

"I've a mind to put it to the test, you know."

"Test what?"

"The difference between her then and now."

"That's going a bit far, too. Makes you sound like a professional student of lesbianism. The trouble is, probably, you think Maki sounds a bit too

self-satisfied with her talk about 'we women' and the like.''

"*Self-satisfied, eh? True enough—perhaps what I'd like is to drag her away from the world of 'we women' and rough her up a bit.*"

At this point Maki broke in.

"What's wrong? You're so quiet."

"I was just taking in what you said," I replied, and switched to a more flippant vein. "Men, I assume, aren't allowed to see the lake?"

"Let me see. . . . They can't *swim* in the lake, but they can see it, I suppose."

"Ah! Inspection without participation. D'you think you could arrange a viewing?"

"Yes, of course. But I'm not sure what the other girl would say. I'll ask."

"Why should you want to be seen, though?"

Maki's expression went vague.

"Anyway, shall we go?" I got up as I spoke. Maki got up with me, then hesitated and said,

"But where?"

"You don't need to inquire, do you?"

Outside, she spoke again:

"What made you ask me to come tonight?"

"Do you hate the idea?"

"I don't feel anything either way."

The reply, it occurred to me, was just right, coming from the woman who'd written those notes. I set off and she took her place silently by my side. My idea was to go to a hotel, and I felt sure she'd accompany me without objecting.

27

This was the third time I'd seen Maki naked. I recalled the urge to assault her I'd felt a while earlier, but now, beside her naked body, I was more dispassionate. I gazed at her with the eyes of a detached observer. She seemed to have got slightly slimmer round the waist, but the muddy color of the skin, as though it had been given a thin coating of gray, was the same as before.

Even when Maki was in bed, the bright gleam in her eyes remained unveiled, reminding you all the time of her sharp intelligence.

"About those notes you wrote, I can't help feeling—," I began, perfectly aware as I did so that the subject was out of place.

Maki said nothing.

"I get the idea you left off halfway. I just don't feel it's the kind of piece that should end with a discussion of fellatio."

"It was just that one of the girls actually met a man who boasted he'd had a lesbian go down on him."

"You mean that part didn't have any special significance?"

I still felt that something about what Maki had written suggested a greater interest than the explanation she'd just given. But quite suddenly she launched into another subject.

"I'm going to America at the end of the summer. There's only two months left."

"Oh. Still, I suppose lots of people make trips abroad these days."

"It's not a trip. It's for four years. I'm going to New York to study interior decoration."

"Four years? That's a long while. It means we won't be able to see each other for some time."

"I had a feeling that once I said I was going abroad I'd be brought to a place like this again. But in fact it happened even before I said anything. So I can't understand why you were so standoffish while we were away together. . . . I think you must be a bit of a sadist."

"I'm no sadist."

"Mentally, I mean."

"And you thought I might gratify my sadism by making you blow me, did you? I suppose what you wrote was a kind of self-justification in advance, in case it happened."

"No, it wasn't. It's nothing to do with self-justification. Didn't you read what I wrote?"

"What exactly did you write? . . ."

"That our relations with men have nothing to do with sex. That we lose the ability to feel any emotion in sex with a man."

"If it's nothing to do with sex, what about us at the moment?"

"I know, but there's no real sex in this."

"Then why do you have to let it happen at all?"

"Because this is how the man wants it. . . . Personally, I dislike it."

"You're being self-sacrificing?"

"That's right."

"I don't get it."

"You wouldn't. You're not even trying."

"Of course I am. I think what mixes things up is when you don't realize the gap between what you feel consciously and unconsciously."

"But—"

She looked as if she was going to raise some objection, but I stopped her.

"That's enough of this talk," I said. "As I thought," I added just to clinch things, "you're all confused. You don't know your own mind."

As I spoke, I got on top of her. It occurred to me that this was probably the first time I'd spouted psychology as I got into position for intercourse. The idea tickled me.

When I'd made love to her before, her body had stayed still while her head twisted sharply from side to side on the bed. One moment her right ear would appear, then the left, so that the gold balls fastened in the lobes flashed on and off. She seemed to be clenching her teeth. Perhaps she'd been a virgin, as Yuzuru said.

This time, the idea that I was forcing her excited me. I kept my eyes on her face. It stayed still. The heavy makeup sat on it motionless as a mask.

Time passed, but her head didn't move.

"Is it nice?" I whispered in her ear. It was the unconscious urge to be the rapist that made me say it. But there wasn't much in her expression that suggested pleasure. I was reflecting ruefully on this when she said,

"Yes, it's nice."

The voice didn't sound as though it cost her any particular effort. But it wasn't a straightforward sort of voice, either. It had what you might call a faked naturalness. Her face, eyes closed, was as like a mask as ever. A sense of uneasiness brushed my mind.

"Why?" I heard myself ask.

"Why?" she echoed. The voice came out cool and collected. The eyes opened. Gaze met gaze. She shut her eyes immediately, parted her lips slightly, and gave a faint moan. The effect was artificial, perhaps, but the artifice was too naive to upset things for me. Unwilting, I pressed on to the end.

28

For several days after I parted from Maki, the two brief words we'd exchanged would crop up in my mind from time to time then disappear again, like two small bulbs flashing on and off:

"Why?"

"Why?"

I chuckled to myself every time it happened. But sometimes the interrogation brought another question in its wake:

"Why should Maki have been lying underneath me then?"

I couldn't say. There were several possible answers, but I couldn't be sure which was the right one.

It was nearly two months later that I got a reply from Maki over the phone. It coincided with none of the possible answers I'd thought up:

"I'm pregnant."

It came without preliminaries; I thought perhaps I'd misheard.

"Uh? What did you say?"

"I'm going to have a kid."

I just couldn't associate pregnancy and lesbianism. Even so, when I made love to her I'd checked, in a whisper, to make sure she was in a safe period.

"What will you . . .?"

"What will I . . .?"

"You've got to get rid of it!"

"No, I'm going to have it."

I was at a loss for a moment. For several seconds the telephone stayed silent.

"Hello?" came Maki's voice. It was hard for me to gauge the quality that tinged her voice.

"Either way, we'll have to see each other," I said.

"I can't make it. I'm leaving for New York tomorrow, so I'm busy getting ready."

At last I found my tongue.

"But surely, isn't having a kid a betrayal of your crowd?"

"Not at all." The reply was prompt, the voice cool. "We all look after the kids as they grow up. There's a similar kind of community in New York, so it shouldn't be difficult to bring up mine."

"I don't get it," I said, aloud. "I just don't understand your world . . . or at least, your way of thinking."

But she might be lying: the idea hadn't occurred to me till then.

"Don't have it," I said in a tone of feigned unconcern.

"I'm going to."

"But I have half the rights where the kid's concerned, don't I?"

"OK—then I'll let you see it after a few years. You'd like that, wouldn't you?"

"I'm not interested in seeing it."

"Just as you like. . . . I know, you see, that you don't believe in having children."

"Then I wish you'd get rid of it."

"Children are just born, it isn't anyone's responsibility. Besides, I'm not asking you to support it financially; I'll be bringing it up because I want to, so you needn't worry."

It could well be a lie, I told myself firmly, and changed the subject. We made desultory conversation for a while, till finally I said,

"Well, have a good time then," and hung up.

I remembered something suddenly. The first time I went to an inn with Maki, I'd picked up a short, sharp, glittering gold pin off the sheet. Part of Maki's earring. Maki had taken it carefully from between my fingers, and our nails had touched lightly. I'd felt a fine line linking us: a fine line, not a fine *gold* line.

She might be lying or she might not. But what lay behind it all? Had I invited Maki to accompany me on the trip just at a time when she wanted to restore her ties with men? If so, then her behavior could be seen as either mockery or revenge, depending on the strength of that desire.

"Revenge" is a strong word, but for me at least the matter justified it. What about Maki herself, though—could a lesbian really have a child out of sheer spite? Or perhaps having a child was purely a matter of maternal instinct, something quite unassociated with men? . . .

29

Late one night, Tsunoki called me. He'd already called several times to remind me about the manuscript. But on each occasion I'd begged more time. Not that he himself had sounded all that pressing.

"It's all up with Maki," I said.

"I suppose so, now she's so far away."

He knew she'd left, then. Perhaps he'd talked to her about me.

"So it's no good," I reiterated, trying to prod him on. He might know whether Maki was really pregnant or not.

I was afraid he might reply, "Actually, it's more promising with her out of the way, isn't it?" But he said,

"Can't be helped. You can't do anything without the material to work on. What I wanted to say, though, was that we haven't seen you around town much recently. Health not too good?"

"It's better than it was, at least."

"It won't do—all work and no play, you know. Come on out!"

"*Now?*" I looked at my watch. Nearly twelve.

"I know an interesting spot."

His usual ploy. A few drinks wouldn't hurt, I reflected.

The place we were taken to was in a modern ferroconcrete building. A number of men and women were sitting drinking on the floor, which was covered with a deep purple carpet. The room was cramped, and we found ourselves squashed against strangers of both sexes. Overcoming my distaste, I exchanged conventional remarks with Tsunoki as I drank.

All of a sudden, I heard a sound like sobbing.

Two bodies lay entangled on the floor. A pair of legs protruding from a short skirt were entwined with another pair in narrow slacks. But a closer look revealed the couple were both women.

I felt a spasm of disgust. Why did one of them have to get herself up as a man? The other woman, who lay on her back, unhooked her skirt and removed her blouse with caressing motions, till finally she lay naked. Her body was slim but well-fleshed, and reminded me of Natsue. It stood out white under the dim lights. The oval face with the finely molded nose was heavily made up. In a way, she was beautiful.

"Is this staged?" I asked Tsunoki.

"Staged?"

"Do they employ women here to put on a show?"

"Of course not. They're customers like the rest."

"Lesbians, then?"

"I suppose so."

"But why in front of people?"

"I imagine they're drunk."

The second woman removed her slacks, exposing her lower half. She stretched out beside the woman lying on her back, then drew closer and placed a hand on her belly.

There followed the various techniques that women use in each other's arms. All the while, sounds like sobs and moans. The sounds were utterly feminine, and I assumed they came exclusively from the woman who was naked. But I was wrong. Two voices of similar timbre were superimposed on each other.

Suddenly the second woman sat up and removed her upper garment, which was like a man's shirt. The two of them fell into each other's arms and, tightly clasped together, sank to the floor. The woman who'd been wearing slacks was just as fair-skinned as the other. She was slender and supple; even her height was almost the same.

"Beautiful!" whispered Tsunoki.

"The lake," I thought as I watched.

The two bodies lay motionless, firmly entwined, almost as though they'd fused into a single mass. Four breasts, pushed out of shape between tightly embracing bodies. Suddenly the bodies began to look unnatural in my eyes. The white flesh seemed stained the same color as the carpet: four arms and four legs, protruding from a single, deep purple body.

The single body had two heads.

30

One day in summer found me on board a plane, a domestic flight. The "Fasten Seat Belts" sign went on, and I lifted my eyes from my magazine. To go on looking at the shaking print made me feel unpleasantly queasy.

I gazed out of the window. We were flying over the sea. The water, innocent of the turbulence above, was an even indigo undisturbed by a single white breaker. On the calm surface a small green island appeared and began slowly to retreat toward the rear.

A while later I looked out of the window again, down at the sea, and got a shock.

We were directly above the green island. In the shape of a ring with one small segment missing, it was covered with dense trees that gave it its attractive color. But around the inside of the circle enclosing the water, as though embedded in it, I could see a close rank of small, narrow objects. I soon realized that they were fishing boats, lined up flank to flank on the beach where dark gray sand formed a border between island and water. But even after I'd realized it, the scene refused to look that way.

The effect was vile.

A monstrous beast lay there, green lips agape. The oral cavity was indigo-colored, and from gums the hue of mud projected a jagged row of small, dirty-brown teeth.

I followed the slowly shifting island with my eyes till eventually the inside of the ring disappeared from sight and it became a beautiful green island once more.

I was suddenly reminded of Takako. To me she'd always seemed a pleasant woman, and there were no jarring memories of her. But I suspected now that I'd been so determined not to let us get too closely involved that I'd promptly dismissed from my mind any slight abrasions she inflicted on it.

A number of unpleasant recollections began to stir in me.

I wondered if Takako hadn't hated me in one part of her mind. During the first two years of our relationship, we'd met at inns and I'd shown no interest in going to her apartment. A room in an inn has a bathroom and toilet, but no kitchen. Personally I liked that aspect of it, and my affection for such places may have hurt Takako. It was probably around then that she'd realized I didn't have a family.

Finally, during the last two years, I began to go to Takako's apartment. As familiarity with her gradually made me lower my guard, it had begun to seem too much trouble to make a date and go to an inn every time. But in fact, I suspected, this had been a mistake.

Takako began consciously to look to the future. Despite the change of place, though, my own attitude didn't change in the slightest. I'm sure she hated me for that, though it may only have been unconscious.

On a very few occasions during those four years, Takako had failed to show up at the appointed place. I'd gone to her apartment, only to find her out and be forced, finally, to beat a retreat from her unyielding door.

The first time she broke our appointment, I stayed on for a while, sitting in the coffee shop where we'd arranged to meet, looking vacantly in front of me. The odor of Takako's body was faint, almost imperceptible. But as the perfume she put on her skin got warm, she gave off a characteristic smell. As I sat there alone my nostrils seemed to catch, unmistakably, a whiff of her body, and I almost felt I might be in love with her. I wondered what could have kept her, worried in case there'd been an accident—wondered too, with a feeling of suspicion, what she could be doing.

In the end I decided to go to an inn where they had girls on call. I felt it as a kind of duty to my unsettled emotions. And in fact, as soon as I was in bed with the woman—a complete stranger—the jarring emotions inside me vanished immediately.

"That'll show you!" I thought.

From then on, whenever Takako didn't keep an appointment, I made a beeline for the inn.

It made my mind easy to feel I could dispose of things that way. Takako may have sensed how I felt, and allowed a part of her to hate me for it.

The light went out behind the "Fasten Seat Belts" sign, and my eyes turned back to the print again; but still the ring-shaped thing I'd seen wouldn't leave my mind.

I still couldn't see it as an island. It was a nameless, threatening object that conveyed a sense of evil.

"Evil"—I'd come out with the same word, I recalled, at a discussion among a group of authors sponsored by a magazine. I struggled to remember bits of the conversation we'd had.

"A man's sex organs are relatively frank and straightforward," I'd said, "but a vagina has something very evil about it, for me at least. If I could only see it as—say—a rose, like some people, I'd be overjoyed. The only impression it makes on me is of something evil."

"That's typical of you," said someone.

"Let's hear more about this theory of evil," said someone else.

"You can hardly call it a theory," I said. "I'd just like to achieve a state where something evil could look like a rose."

"I'm sure we're all the same, in practice."

"Tell me, Nakata," put in another, "how would you set about making it look like a rose?"

As I remembered it, I'd replied simply, "I'm sure it would be a tough job," and people laughed.

I hadn't meant it negatively, as an indication of resignation. It seemed to me that this talk of reaching a state of mind where evil looked like a flower had been more than a passing turn of phrase. The desire, I realized now, had been lurking in me all the while I'd been longing for a life free from the bother of women. Yet to satisfy it

112

required that one should be deeply involved with them. I wasn't sure even now what kind of involvement would produce my rose, but I wondered if perhaps I still had a lingering wish to try.

During the past six months the women about me had disappeared one by one.

Yumiko had gone, then Takako. Both in order to get married.

Maki had left too. Left announcing she was going to have my kid and bring it up in a foreign country. By now, I saw the announcement as a mockery of me. Her lesbianism was probably only a fraud after all—not that I knew, when I thought about it, what a "genuine" homosexual was, unless it implied inability to escape from homosexuality as a "symptom". . . . I wouldn't have been in the least surprised to hear that Maki had got married abroad.

The only survivor was Natsue.

The thing I liked about my relationship with Natsue was that I didn't have to bother about being responsible. My senses, too, were titillated by the mildly stimulating situations that acquaintance with her occasionally involved me in. But my attitude to her could never be anything but negative.

This feeling was seriously at variance with my remarks during that discussion. Had I just been talking nonsense, then? I couldn't believe so.

31

I looked up the discussion in the magazine when I got back from my trip. The exchange following the part I'd remembered went as follows:

> *Nakata*: A tough job, no doubt about it. [Laughter]
> *K*: Do you mean you've actually felt it so, or that you feel it will be from now on?

Nakata: From now on. I'm just considering the question at the moment.

Y: Yes, it would be tough. But personally I don't find the thing as evil as all that. For me, you see, it's just something with hair round it—you know? So I'm not all *that* against it. [Laughter]

K: I'm the same, my approach is more *relaxed*. . . . [Laughter] In Nakata's case, though, I suspect he's always felt the same way. I've tried all kinds of ways of accounting for it—the Freudian approach, for example.

Y: Yes, I can't help seeing it in Freudian terms too. Some childhood experience. . . .

Nakata: Sorry to disappoint you, but there wasn't one. [Laughter]

Y: But you just can't explain it in any other way.

O: Why not let Nakata pursue the question in his own way? Without Freud. . . .

The discussion was for a literary magazine, but conversation always takes this turn as soon as I open my mouth. I gave Y's doubts some more thought, but came up with nothing. I never played "doctor" when I was a kid, and I reached my late teens without exchanging even the briefest conversation with a girl of my own age. Not from any phobia, I suspect, but from overawareness of the other sex. . . .

Keiko was the first woman I knew. Considered in Freudian terms, everything could be traced back to her. I had a vision of Tsunoki's face. I shoved it out of the way, along with Freud's face. I knew Freud's face from a photograph. It was taken in the last years before he died at eighty-three; the impression was of very classical features—white hair carefully parted on one side above the oval face, firmly set lips, neatly trimmed mustache and beard. . . . The beard and mustache were white too. A fine face, with a broad nose, and a sharp light in the eyes betraying a strong will. In the photograph, at least, he wasn't wearing glasses.

The following day, I had an unexpected call to say they were preparing a new edition of a collection of my essays published three years earlier. The book had been full of misprints, and I was reading it over so that I could get them corrected, when I came across the following passage. I'd completely forgotten it, though I'd written it myself:

> Throughout the ages, there seems to have been some special fate linking children and maids. One often hears, for example, of children being interfered with by the family maid. I myself was looked after by a young maid who exactly fitted the hackneyed expression "fat as a pig." The strongest recollection I have of her is of finding her one day bawling her head off in the dark emptiness of the barn that stood next to the garden. Beside her stood my grandfather—a mulish old man, who was whispering something in a, for him, unusually gentle tone. He was obviously trying to soothe her. That was all, but it gave me an uncomfortable, grotesque feeling. Something about the incident obviously lodged in my sexual awareness with a discordant note. I learned later that the maid in question had been my grandfather's mistress.
>
> I don't say that this incident set things off—the real cause, I'm sure, lay in my own disposition—but when I was a boy the mere proximity of a girl was enough to set my sexual sensibilities jangling. I got tense and awkward—partly because I had no means of showing that interest in a more relaxed way.

32

When we'd landed in Shikoku and I'd finished my business in the area, I set off for the San'in district: for the same small town that I'd been to with Maki.

An uncle of mine lived there. He was in his mid-fifties, but still got involved with women. What made it more complicated was the smallness of the town, since people talked. As a boy he'd been a tough little guy who was forever getting into fights, and had been expelled four times from middle school. Even now, if he came up to Tokyo and swaggered through the streets, aggressively at home in his loose kimono, wooden clogs, and dark glasses, young hoods would mistake him for a gang boss and bow as he passed.

We were talking of things in general when he said,

"Can't seem to find a wife for the boy."

"How old is he now?"

"Thirty."

"He doesn't need to get married just yet, does he?"

"But you see, his section chief keeps pressing him to find a wife. In a big office people don't seem to trust you if you stay single too long."

"I suppose not."

It was natural enough if you thought about it, but he'd put his finger on a sore spot.

"So all the trouble starts again," I said.

"You could put it that way. But parents and children have their own lives to lead, you know."

True enough, I thought. Even so, the upshot would be another married couple and, before long, children. It was all very well, but . . . I was idly turning things over in my mind when my uncle said,

"Anyway, how about going out for a drink?"

He got up ponderously. His apartment was on the fourth floor of a ferroconcrete block, but there was no elevator. His corpulent belly stuck out solemnly in front of him as he preceded me down the narrow stairs, and his shoes echoed with a dull, hard ring.

I had nearly reached the bottom of the stairs when I heard his ripe voice say:

"Hello, there! Been out to play?"

In the narrow passageway, he was patting a small girl affectionately on the head. She came roughly up to his waist, and had a round face with a fringe.

The child brushed past me, and I heard her halting footsteps climbing the stairs.

She probably belonged to a family in the same building. My uncle was standing waiting for me at the entrance. The passage was rather too narrow for us to stand side by side, but he didn't move. As I stopped, just behind him and to one side, he said without turning round,

"That's the best age for a woman."

Then in a quiet voice like a sigh he murmured, as though half to himself,

"When they get bigger—dear, oh dear. . . ."

And he set off heavily, walking slowly, with a slightly bandy gait. I watched his wide trousers flapping, then turned my gaze upward. The evening sky was not rosy with sunset, but a dim ivory that held a minimum of light. A sky without gradations, as though it had been sprayed evenly all over with the same color.

33

Back in Tokyo, I called Natsue. I never let the phone ring more than six times. I waited in vain for the sound of the receiver being lifted.

After about an hour I called again, with the same result. The next day and the day after, the same state of affairs continued. Normally, I knew, she'd answer the phone even when her lover was there.

Suddenly, I could hear her voice saying again: "I'm thinking of moving."

What had been behind the remark? If it meant she was going somewhere where I couldn't find her, then my only remaining woman had gone. I ran over the conversation we'd had at the time:

"I'm thinking of moving."

"Moving?"

"Yes. How about it?"

"Mightn't be a bad idea."

I remember replying rather vaguely. What she'd said didn't seem to imply that she was going to stop seeing me.

I waited to see if she'd contact me from her side. There was no alternative.

Physically, I was impatient for her. I was just getting to the end of a longish piece of work, so I did most of the waiting at home. Sometimes, when I got stuck over a phrase, I'd put my pen down, let my mind go blank, and the various physical characteristics of her body would rise up in my mind:

The amber skin, growing damp with sweat. . . .

The soft pliancy of the body that had something tough and resilient at its core. . . .

The varied positions, adopted with no hint of shame. . . .

The low, rather husky, sensually troubling voice. . . .

Once, when these fragments of memory began to stir, I thought of visiting the inn where they had girls on call, and I even started to get up from my chair. If I told the madame just what I wanted, it shouldn't be hard to find a woman who'd do in place of Natsue.

But in the end I sat down again: partly because of pressure of work, but also, I suspect, because of a kind of premonition (whether I felt this at the time or only later isn't clear).

I went out into the garden for the first time in ages. There was a natural spring, and a narrow stream flowing from it, with cress growing by its side. The flowering season was past, but one single stalk bore a small, cross-shaped white flower at the top. This stalk was thin, but the others were thick and sturdy, with dark green leaves sprouting all over.

I noticed that the leaves had tiny holes in them. I crouched down to get a closer look, and found a mass of small black insects. Almost too small to be living creatures, they looked like specks of soot scattered over the leaves. They seemed hard and dry, yet I felt they'd stick to your hand if you touched them. A wasp with a single gold stripe on its long, swollen abdomen hovered in the air by the perforated leaves, its wings beating busily.

I got up and called to the girl who came in to help with the housework. (Since Yumiko left, I'd taken on a boyish-looking girl in her teens.)

"Would you go and buy some insecticide, please?"

There was a small pond that Yumiko had had made without asking me and filled with water from the stream. I crouched down again and peered into the water; a large, straw-colored worm rose vertically from the bed, swaying to and fro, as though it grew out of the moss-covered concrete. There was no other life. The water was quite clear.

"Wait—," I called after the girl, who was just going out of the gate. "Get me some killifish while you're about it."

"OK," she called back. "How many d'you want?"

"A hundred—no, a hundred and fifty."

I disliked goldfish. I found them too fat-bellied, dank, and fishy. If I were forced to keep goldfish under pain of death, I'd choose the black, pop-eyed kind.

As fish go, though, I'm quite fond of killifish. They have a dried-up, non-fleshy look. When goldfish in a bowl die, they rise to the surface with their white, swollen bellies turned uppermost and the reek of death about them. Killifish have no taint of the flesh, even in death.

The girl came back carrying a transparent plastic bag. Small and full of water, it was crammed with killifish like short pieces of orange thread.

My spirits perked up. I opened the top of the bag and poured the contents into the pond. Though the movement didn't feel particularly violent, it was vigorous enough to dash the contents of the bag against the surface of the pond.

The next moment, a hundred and fifty killifish lay on the bottom of the pond, their bellies turned upward or to one side. Lying there in a densely packed layer, they had that unmistakable "raw" look. It was a shock.

The phrase "piles of corpses" came into my mind. (I soon realized what it was they'd stirred up in my subconscious. May 25, 1945— the night of the last great air raid on Tokyo. I'd stood watching the sky without going into the shelter, and two objects fell one on either side of me about five yards away. An incendiary bomb, and one of the thick iron cylinders that hold bundles of incendiaries. The bomb itself, as I realized when I returned to the ruins the next morning, had not exploded. Someone told me that at Miyamasuzaka the ground was covered with an unbroken layer of corpses; though when I walked through a couple of days later they'd already been cleared away. . . .)

Suddenly, three or four of the killifish roused themselves and began swimming. I strained my eyes to see the bottom of the pool, wondering if the shock of hitting the water had merely stunned them. Here and there, I could see fish feebly stirring their fins. As I watched, some of them showed their backs and began to swim. With others, the movement of the fins came to a halt.

I stayed crouched by the pond watching this for quite a while. At the end, about a hundred of them were still lying there motionless.

34

On the fifth day, there was a call from Natsue. I'd given her my number just in case, but (another thing I liked about her) she'd never used it before.

Today, the normally low voice was faint and husky to the point of inaudibility.

"I nearly died." It sounded like that, but I couldn't be sure.

"What? Speak up a bit, will you?"

"I nearly died." This time I got it quite clearly.

"A traffic accident?"

I was a little startled, but my first response was to wonder whether a certain part of her body hadn't been damaged.

"No. I was almost murdered."

"Come off it."

"But it's *true*."

Her voice had no overtone of excitement, nor did it suggest the indifference of despair. It was the faint cry of a small insect lying there curled up and still.

"What happened, for God's sake?"

"I moved house."

I began vaguely to understand. But it still left a lot unclear.

"So? . . ."

"I mean, I made a run for it."

"By moving?"

"That's right. And he found me. He nearly beat me to death. On and on. . . . I really thought I was being murdered. You should've seen the mad look in his eyes as he came at me."

It was a long speech, but the tone stayed just as faint and uninflected.

I was silent.

"That's the kind of man he is," Natsue said.

"And? . . ."

"And then he let me off."

"Just like that?"

"That's typical, too. But you can never be sure. So I moved again."

"You mean, you've moved twice?"

"He won't find me this time."

"How did he find you before?"

"Because he tried to."

I suddenly remembered the big double bed in Natsue's room.

"What did you do with the bed?"

"Uh? The bed? I got rid of it. I've got a new, smaller one in its place."

"The first time you moved—?"

"I took it with me."

"That's how he found you."

The great wooden bed was firmly installed in my mind: square, massive, exclusive. The wood, saturated with male and female odors, was a thin shell concealing a soft, syrupy interior. It smelled.

"The bastard!" Then, before I had time to wonder why I should feel that way about Natsue's lover, I heard myself say accusingly,

"Why didn't you get rid of the bed when you moved?"

Her voice began to recover some inflection.

"I chucked out all the small things. Even the slippers and my toothbrush. But I couldn't leave the bed there, and it was too big to throw out. . . . After all, I moved in a hurry, at half a day's notice. Even so . . . you're right—it was the bed that gave me away."

Something in the words suggested a different Natsue from the one I thought I knew.

"Can you get around?"

"No, I can't, I'm stretched out half dead. My face is still all lop-sided."

"It's a wonder you managed to move house."

"I only just made it. That makes me all the more . . . I never want to see him again!"

"Didn't you say he'd forgiven you?"

"He wouldn't beat me up again, but he might come to see me. He kept accusing me of having another man, he said he'd let me off if I told him. . . . But I said no I hadn't, right to the end."

This puzzled me. I'd thought she'd had all kinds of other men. Was Natsue going to be the woman I finally got involved with, then? I was beginning to feel depressed when she went on,

"I didn't care if he killed me. Even so . . . he forgave me. But if he found it was a lie . . . Can I see you?"

A nice fix, I thought. My relationship with Natsue was supposed to have been "safe." But to abandon her now, I told myself (deliberately using the old-fashioned word), would be "unmanly."

35

A few days after hearing that Natsue had moved, I finished the fairly lengthy manuscript I'd been working on. For just one day, I had the sense of release of a man staggering under a heavy load who's finally got it to its destination. The day after that, the cheerfulness steadily went over into gloom, and my condition, both physical and mental, suddenly began to go downhill. I'd always been a bit of a manic-depressive, but now the depressive side began to get the upper hand.

It was summer, but even on fine, relatively dry days I felt as though my whole being was waterlogged. The food on my plate looked heavy and greasy, and I could hardly bring myself to touch it. Even pale-colored foods looked chalky, as though they'd stick to the roof of my mouth.

I wasn't quite sure how this lapse related to Natsue. But of one thing I was certain. From the moment I decided to protect my "manliness," I felt I'd got one foot in the mire: I could almost feel the sticky slime oozing through the four fine cracks between my toes.

I wish I could be more callous toward others. Not only do I get into awkward positions myself, but I sometimes bring down trouble on the other person's head as well. The same thing applied, I realize now, where Keiko, my dead wife, was concerned. There are times when such an attitude is better for both concerned, even if it looks like cowardice. But for me that's not possible. It was particularly impossible to turn my back on Natsue at a time like this, when I knew she needed me. With eyes open, I walked toward the swamp that I knew lay ahead.

When Natsue asked if she could see me, I went. She was scared, and stayed scared all the way to the hotel. She shrank into a corner of the taxi, practically lying on the seat so as not to be seen from outside.

"From now on, I'm coming to your place," I said once we were in the room.

"I thought you never went to a woman's place?"

I had a momentary vision of Takako's apartment. It had been on the plane to Shikoku that I'd resolved never to go to a woman's apartment again.

"It can't be helped, it seems."

"But you'd feel uneasy, wouldn't you?"

I took this to refer to the possibility of her lover's getting wind of her new address.

"We can cross that bridge when we come to it."

I started visiting her at her own place, but it bothered me every time there was a footstep outside the door or the phone rang.

But there'd been another meaning to Natsue's "you'd feel uneasy."

During my third or fourth visit she said, glancing round the tiny room with its narrow bed squeezed up against the wall,

"I know why you can't settle down here."

I said nothing.

"It's because I *live* here, isn't it?"

This was unexpected. It's true, I never feel settled in the kind of feminine room that reeks of ordinary, everyday life.

In the back of my mind, I gave her full marks for perspicacity. But I just nodded and kept quiet. My mental image of her had changed still further.

But though for a while our conversations were longer, we soon began to talk even less than before. I'd come to feel it was a nuisance that Natsue should be different from what I'd believed her to be. My physical and mental state made the feeling all the stronger.

I stopped going out into town, and went to Natsue's room instead. We had almost no connected conversation, but we let ourselves go physically. A feeling lurking inside me—a feeling that once this became impossible, I'd reached the end of the road—drove me to Natsue's room again and again.

For a considerable period of time, Natsue's room continued to depress me in the double sense. But it never occurred to me to invite her to my place.

36

The best part of a year passed with no relief for my low spirits.

Real work was impossible during that period. I wrote odd things here and there to earn enough to keep me going, but I didn't need much. It cost me little to live, since I never went out, didn't drink, and ate sparingly. And with the occasional royalties on new editions of earlier works of mine, I even managed to save.

Once, I tried to give Natsue money. I was careful about the way I did it, of course, but I never expected there'd be any difficulty.

"I don't need it," she said. Lots of women say that the first time, I thought. But she persisted:

"Really, it's all right."

"But since you've lost your rich lover . . ."

"Rich lover?—you're the one who used the phrase, not me."

"I didn't, it was you."

"Really? . . . It must've just slipped out. Actually, there wasn't much money involved between us."

"Then he was just a lover, was he?"

"If we'd loved each other, I wouldn't have run out on him like that."

"Then what was it?"

"A convenience. A sexual convenience."

"For which side?"

"Which side?" She hesitated. "Both of us."

I wasn't prepared to accept this at its face value. If I did, what did it make her relationship with me?

"I'd like to know how you make a living, though."

For a moment, I was aware again of the strong odor her body gave off. It had occurred to me once that it was the smell of the mingled secretions of many different men, seeping out through her flesh, becoming one with the perfume that she used to excess as camouflage. . . . And yet, Natsue somehow didn't seem like a whore.

"I don't need much money," she said. "I don't go anywhere, and I eat hardly anything."

At most, I'd seen Natsue nibbling at hard, dry things like pieces of chocolate, or sipping at some liquid in a glass.

"But it was at a food store I first met you."

"So it was. A food store. . . ."

Reminiscence overtook me. I'd stopped by the store to get some wine, and my eyes had met those of a young woman.

I caught my breath in surprise. It rarely happens to me, but something told me at once that I could make this woman. By nature, though, I'm not the type who can speak to a completely strange woman. So far, I'd never once done it. (I'm only talking about one aspect of my nature, the part that can't make advances to a woman in that particular way.)

I looked away again immediately, and left the store carrying my wine as soon as it was wrapped.

Toward evening about two weeks later, I came round the corner of the street and saw a woman there, standing in front of me looking down at the ground.

"Hello, there!" I said, just as I might have done if I'd bumped into an acquaintance.

The next moment, I realized it was the woman whose eyes had met mine in the supermarket. She looked up at me without speaking, a smile around her lips. For a moment, I had a feeling she'd suddenly materialized out of the ground.

Her whole body seemed to beckon to me. I rested a hand on her shoulder.

"Let's go," I said. My words could have been taken in various ways, but she replied,

"I can't today. Another time."

"Another time? And when will that be?"

Her hair was just about on a level with my chin. A strong, troubling scent reached me.

"Let's go," I said, almost automatically. "I'm sure we've got things in common."

By "in common," I meant something like, "we're neither of us quite respectable anyway, so let's have some fun, without getting all uptight about it."

I'd certainly covered a lot of ground between the slight start I gave on seeing her a couple of weeks earlier and what I'd just said. It was her smell, I think, that gave me the courage.

So here she was with me now, the woman whose name was Natsue. And talking of names . . . My next question, I feel, must have been tinged with surprise:

"Of course—I meant to ask you. What's your surname?"

The same smile played about her mouth as when I'd found her standing at the street corner.

"I wondered when you'd get around to that."

"You were hoping I would?"

"Not hoping, just wondering when. Have you heard the name —?" She gave the name of a small town in the country.

"That's unusual as a surname."

"It's not my surname. We were talking about how I support myself. Well, my family send me money every month to help me out, and that's the name of the place where they live."

"Help you out? Then what do you live on basically?"

"I went to design school. So I manage to get by doing fashion pictures and sketches—at least, that's what my parents believe."

Or pretend to believe, I thought. I saw a serried rank of men's heads lined up behind Natsue: faces unknown to me, the vaguest of outlines filled in with black. Their part in her life was over, but they still felt concerned and sent money. . . . If I were to hint that that was the true story, Natsue would probably shrug it off with a cool "maybe."

"But it's true it doesn't cost me much to live," she said. "So I just about survive on what they send me."

I believed her—seventy per cent, at least.

"All right, I know. What about your surname, though?"

"Yashiro."

"Natsue Yashiro," I repeated to myself; but the family name slipped my mind again almost immediately. Even her first name, Natsue, I'd never once uttered aloud. Often enough, it too disappeared entirely, leaving only the reality of her body.

37

A year passed in which I didn't buy a single book. People sent me books and magazines, but I was too washed out to read all but a few of them.

One day, I noticed on my desk a collection of photographs in black and white. Quite obviously I'd unwrapped it and put it there myself, but it often happened nowadays that I forgot something I'd done only a few minutes earlier. I opened its pages idly enough, but soon my attention was riveted.

This time, I had a feeling that some unseen hand must have deposited the book unnoticed on my desk. I went through it thoroughly, page by page. That done, I was to open it again only occasionally, as the fancy took me, but each time I found it as gripping as ever. For a whole year, in fact, it was as though I was shuttling to and fro between the book of photos and Natsue's body. So I'll go into its contents in rather more detail.

The book began with a bare four pages of text, which seemed to be some kind of commentary but which, since it was in German, I couldn't read.

The cover was black, with the word for "woman" in sixteen languages arranged in white rows on the black background. There were photographs, bordered in white, of four women—one white, one yellow, and one black, with another white woman who looked like a German.

The collection consisted of 522 photographs of the female, from babes in arms to old hags, from all parts of the world. None of the photos had any caption apart from the woman's nationality and the name of the photographer.

Some pages carried only one photo, others as many as six or seven together. The editor of the collection seemed to have done a good job.

There was a Brazilian infant with arms that looked as though the skin was stretched directly over the bones. Her right arm was crooked, and the fingers of the hand placed against the chest looked unnaturally large. The breastbone, the collar bones, and the painfully visible ridges of the ribs beneath reminded me exactly of a mummy, but the wide-open eyes were bright and alive. The swollen belly had a protuberant, whorl-shaped navel. The whole picture only took up one-sixth of a page.

There was one shot of thirty-four women in everyday clothes. It was a bird's-eye view, and all the women were looking upward. They were American, all of them young and attractive, but seen from where the camera was they made me feel vaguely apprehensive. They were all in different postures, some sitting on the floor, some seated in chairs, some standing. With thirty-four dank places, tucked away deep between their legs, all looking up at me. . . .

There was just one woman whose body suggested she was pregnant. This one was a full-page photograph. On another page, a smaller photograph caught my attention. A naked woman lay on a flat bench with her knees drawn up and her legs spread as wide as possible. From where her genitals should be a small head projected, face downward: it was the moment when the child in the womb first emerges into the outside air. The left hand of a male doctor grasped the head at the temples. The small face showed no sign of having breathed in new air. The center of the forehead bulged as if the child were still struggling for breath, and the eyes were tightly shut as though swollen from too much weeping.

It was nearly a year after my spiritual and physical decline set in that I called Natsue and said,

"It's all right by now, surely?"

"What?"

"For me to see you eating." I'd first met her shopping for food, but I'd never seen her eat a square meal.

"But—"

"Other things don't embarrass you in the slightest, after all." I told her the restaurant and the time and made her promise to meet me there.

We sat down at the square table, not facing each other, but with

Natsue directly on my right. Unhurriedly, I studied the menu the waiter gave me, and ordered cold consommé.

"I think I'll try the steak tartare," I began.

"Me too," said Natsue promptly.

"It's raw meat, you know."

"Yes, I like it."

After the waiter had gone I said, my eyes fixed on her face, "I shouldn't have thought you'd like that kind of thing."

Her expression changed subtly.

"Here—," I said, "don't put on that face."

"What kind of face is it?"

"Like a cat that's turned itself into a pretty young woman and been caught in the middle of the night, lapping the oil out of the night lamp."

Her expression wavered, but finally settled for silent laughter.

"I meant it in a good sense," I said.

"How can a witch-cat be good, I wonder?"

"I was firmly convinced, you see, that your kind of woman didn't exist. I mean, I don't feel you as a burden at all."

"What's that got to do with witch-cats? . . ."

"I'm convinced that *they* don't exist either. . . . You know, there really was something almost uncanny about it. I'm rather relieved, in fact, to find you've got a stomach that can take steak tartare."

At that moment a young couple came in and sat down at a table some distance from ours. They both looked as though they came from good families, and they seemed to be in love. Both of them were beautiful. They moved with a confident grace, but there was something self-conscious about their behavior that got on my nerves.

"Those two don't really belong here," I said, half to myself. "They're too raw still."

"I hate young couples," said Natsue, who'd caught my remark. "They seem too involved in life." Her tone of voice was offhand.

131

"What's wrong about being involved?"

"Like you said—it's too raw."

"What does that make you, then?"

"I told you, didn't I?—I spend my time just idling about my apartment."

"Yes, I remember. You said that was why I could never settle down in your place."

"It meant something else too, though—that I don't have any real life of my own."

I frowned.

"And what's wrong with that?" she went on. "If I had my own life, it would clash with yours. I'd end up being in the way."

Her next remark came as a jolt:

"After all, you're an egoist."

"Egoist?" I said. "I'd like to meet the man who isn't! Even with people who seem all self-sacrifice, egoism's the real motive. If you're careful enough to make your actions look nice, they often *seem* unselfish to others, but basically they're just the same. . . ."

I hadn't intended to talk to Natsue like this. One thing that had set me off was memories of the war, when the word "egoistic" was synonymous with "unpatriotic." In those days, it would have taken a good deal of courage to announce that I was an egoist.

"I'm an egoist too, of course," she said. "I didn't put it right. What I meant was, I want to give *your* egoism priority."

I said nothing. My frown had meant something different: dismay because I knew that awareness of these feelings in her would make me open up toward her.

It was an awkward situation. The ties between us were supposed to be purely physical. And in some ways it was true that Natsue lived solely for her body. She'd adopt any position I told her to, without a hint of shame. Sometimes she'd say, as if deliberately to incite me, "I used to do anything he wanted me to. . . ."

At the moment, though, she was saying,

"You know, it looks as if I'll never be able to start a baby again. I'm glad."

"Are you *really* glad?"

"Why, do you want a kid?"

"Of course not."

"There you are then—that's why I'm glad," she said.

38

When I got home I took a look at the collection of photographs for the first time in ages.

A young woman lay face up on a bed. She had an attractive body. The wrinkles on the dark bedspread stood out in vivid contrast beneath her white skin. Her face was turned away from the camera, and the shadow behind the one ear formed a sharp line. On a round table in the foreground stood a tall candlestick smothered in melted wax, as though it were festooned with long bunches of tiny grapes.

In very few of the photographs was any man in evidence. Yet with almost all the women one felt a strong male presence in the background. In this very pervasiveness of the male lay the whole significance of the collection.

One photograph showed the bare torso of a black man, with a naked white woman clinging to him from behind. The woman was young and attractive. White fingers and black fingers tangled on the man's shoulder.

As I looked at it, I began to fancy that the woman's face resembled Natsue's. During the past year, I'd been acquiring some fairly detailed information about the numerous men who went before me. As we lay one on top of the other, she would let me have snippets about them. To talk about them made her intensely excited— which fitted in well with my own tastes.

I would ask something, and she'd reply. We'd repeat the process, and as we did so her words would begin to blur, and melt, till only a sound remained.

One whole page was devoted to a naked black woman. She'd struck a pose as though dancing the flamenco, with her body in profile and the light to one side behind her back. The line of the back emerged sharply from the dark page, but the front of the brown body blurred into darkness. One arm was bent, the upper part of it held horizontally at chest level; the other, raised into the air behind the head, was lost in the black background save for the pale undersides of four fingers, which stood out like horns against the black hair. The gleaming teeth were bared.

Another woman, white, had a naked baby in her arms: a boy, with the fair, perfectly smooth skin of infancy. The young mother held her face toward the camera but downturned, with her chin rubbing against the child's temple. The only unusual thing about her was that her body was covered almost entirely with small freckles, so that it seemed to be spotted in brown and black. Folded in her arms, the child looked pure white. Finger and thumb of her right hand gently enclosed the palm of the baby's outthrust left hand. The back of the hand, and even the backs of the fingers, were speckled with black marks.

But the teeth shone white and attractive between lips that parted in a tender smile.

39

It was nearly two years after meeting Natsue that the dismaying realization struck me that I was beginning to let down my barriers toward her.

From around that time, my health began to improve again. And Natsue herself began to seem a different kind of woman.

I don't think that the really essential things in her changed. It was just that they showed themselves in different ways. I suppose, too, that my first contact with her had created a preconception, one that gave a special slant to my view of her ever after. In a way, the change in my own mind had modified the image of Natsue projected on it.

Nevertheless, another transformation, of a completely different nature, had taken place in Natsue physically. In reality, it must have occurred gradually over a period of time, but to me any change I noticed always seemed to have happened overnight.

Natsue's skin had originally been an amber color, but one day I suddenly realized that now it was—not exactly bluish-white, but white behind a colorless, semitransparent film.

"Were you sunburned before?"

"The summer of the year I first met you, I used to lie out on the roof. But not this year."

"I wonder if that's it?"

"No. The basic color of my skin's changed."

"Why?"

"I don't know. You've only just noticed, haven't you?"

"Yes, as a matter of fact."

"I know why you didn't notice before."

I looked at her without saying anything. I hadn't worked out the reason myself yet.

"Because you always dressed and left as soon as you'd finished."

What she apparently meant by this was that while she lay waiting for me, her body would already be flushed a pale pink. Then, before she returned to her normal color, I would already have left her apartment. Even so, I ought to have noticed. It wasn't as if white skin flushing pink was the same as pink seeping up through amber skin. And she hadn't objected to the light in the room, so it wasn't as if it was dark. Come to think of it, it was only recently that I'd begun noticing her new signs of modesty, too.

"You did, you know," she went on. "After all, it's only lately we've started talking to each other."

"*Ordinary* talk, you mean."

I could see her ear flushing red.

"Don't! You make me shy."

This was something new. I told myself that she half meant what she said, and was half saying it to excite herself sexually.

Our two heads were side by side on the bed. When she turned her profile toward me, her ear was just about on a level with my eyes. I stretched out my hand and stroked her behind the ear. My fingertips could feel the wedge-shaped area of bone running toward the top of her skull. The patch of skin here was the only part still suffused with pink. I'd noticed before that this particular area always flushed a remarkably deep red, sometimes to the point where it looked mildly grotesque. But the rosy patch of skin in front of my eyes now began to strike me as rather pathetic.

Experimentally, I put my nose to the area behind the ear. In the past, she'd had a strong, characteristic scent, and I'd expected that even without the drenching perfume a strong body odor would remain. But without perfume Natsue was odorless. I say odorless, yet I sensed about her body a mild fragrance, much as "tasteless" water from a spring has a kind of taste of its own. Somehow it felt like another proof that I was beginning to open up to her.

The same sense of dismay overtook me again. Emotion was reviving in my mind, beginning to prod me into action. I felt wretched at not being able to feel grateful for this development.

I made an effort to change the subject.

"The other week, at that restaurant, you told me you didn't like young couples, didn't you? It struck me that of all the men you've had up to now—"

"It's not all that many."

"It depends on how you set your standards. Anyway, you never mentioned any young men, did you?"

"I don't like them."

"You realize, I suppose, that dislike and indifference aren't the same thing?"

"I'm indifferent."

"Honestly?"

"It's true. You see, I'm not an ordinary woman."

"You're perfectly ordinary."

Natsue had a strong streak of vanity in her. I deliberately made the remark to annoy her.

"Would you like me if I really was an ordinary woman?"

"Well, let's put it differently then. You're an ordinary woman *at heart*."

"But it's true, you know, I've always hated young men."

"Let me explain something that you haven't perhaps realized yourself."

I was reasonably well informed about the men in Natsue's past—even though for almost six months after meeting her, I'd been completely indifferent to the subject. The first man she'd had had been about the same age as myself, with a wife and children. Natsue was eighteen. At one stage they'd set up house together, but in the end the man had gone back to his family.

"I just don't have any sense of possessiveness," Natsue had explained to me. "His wife came to see me and asked for him back, so I let him go."

It was true enough that Natsue had never shown any possessiveness in my case; this was one of the things that had kept our relationship going. But I don't believe there is any human being who is really without the instinct. One just has to avoid anything calculated to bring it into play—which was one reason why I'd felt so much dismay on feeling the first stirrings of emotion.

"That first man, you know—," I went on, "I'm sure you got badly hurt there."

"I suppose so. I went to pieces for a while afterward."

"You mean, the number of men in your life suddenly shot up, don't you?"

"Horrid!"

"There's more to it than that, though," I went on. "All girls around seventeen or eighteen pass through a phase where they fall for middle-aged men. Once it's over, their interest shifts to young men. In your case, it's as though you got so badly hurt in the first phase that you opted out for good. You developed a built-in barrier toward young men."

So here I was, setting out to provide a commentary on the contents of Natsue's subconscious. Even as I spoke, I was marveling at the change in us.

40

I had times when I was glad I'd met Natsue and others when I was sorry. Either way, I told myself, it wasn't all that important. But after another six months, I realized that I was beginning to get deeply involved with her.

From the moment I first met her, a succession of what you might call "coincidences" had worked to keep us together. It was time to do a spot of reconsidering.

"The first time we met, I knew you by sight," she'd once said.

The name Shuichi Nakata is known only to a fairly restricted circle.

"I'm surprised. Did you let yourself get picked up just because I was a writer?"

"No!" she said vehemently. Somewhere in the tone of the denial I sensed a touch of wounded pride. She meant: "I wouldn't do anything so cheap."

Even so, in practice I'd treated her at first like a kind of prostitute. (In the sense of a *safe* woman, a woman who wouldn't involve one in any tedious relationship; in principle, I never normally associate prostitution with cheapness. I don't imagine many women feel the same way, though I suspect that deep down in their subconscious a lot of them have a lingering urge to play the whore.)

It takes all kinds of novelists, too, to make a world. As I see it, the oversensitive and the coarse coexist inside me, and when I said to Natsue, "We've got things in common," it was as though the coarse side of me had sensed in her a kindred spirit.

So I was taken aback when Natsue started talking about the preface to *The Story of O*.

It was during the period following Natsue's second move and the unfortunate incident that occasioned it. Most people assume that the work in question, which was written under the pseudonym "Pauline Réage," is pornographic, so there was nothing surprising about Natsue's having read it. But it was a passage in the lengthy preface that she was pointing to as she said,

"I'm very fond of this part."

I'd read the work myself once and found it something more than mere pornography. But the translation I'd read had omitted the preface.

> "It is true that you make me healthy and happy and a thousand times more alive. Yet there is nothing I can do to prevent this happiness from turning against you. The stone only sings more loudly when the blood flows freely and the body is at rest. Keep me rather in this cage, and feed me sparingly, if you care. Anything that brings me closer to illness and the edge of death makes me more faithful. It is only when you make me suffer that I feel safe and secure. You should never have agreed to be God to me if you were afraid to assume God's duties, and we all know that He is not as tender as all that. You have already seen me cry. Now you must learn to relish my tears. And my neck: is it not charming when, filled with a moan I am striving

to stifle, it grows tense and contorted in spite of my attempts
to control it? It is all too true that when you come to call on
us, you should bring a whip along. And, for more than one
among us, a cat-o'-nine-tails."

When Natsue showed me this passage—barely one page out of
twenty pages of preface—I felt very put out.

"What's this, self-justification?" I ventured, not really meaning
it. But the conversation took its appointed course.

"What do you mean?"

"Justification for the way you've gone from one man to another."

"Not one of them managed to make *me* 'more alive.' That's why
I left them. It's me who left them every time."

This was no real reply to what I'd said. If anything, it smacked
still more strongly of excuses. But I imagined she really believed it,
without any intention of justifying herself. The moment I thought
that, I suddenly saw her as a much misused, rather pitiful girl. I
had a vision of her crouching quite still, smeared all over with the
semen of a horde of lovers. . . .

I decided to read the whole of the preface some day, but now
wasn't the time for heavy reading.

"The word 'God' just doesn't convey anything to me," I said.

"Sometimes she says 'the gods,' in the plural."

"I see. Perhaps it's a kind of master-slave relationship."

I reopened the book, which I'd already closed, and saw that the
preface was entitled "Happiness in Slavery."

"In the course of the year 1838," I read, "the peaceful island of
Barbados was rocked by a strange and bloody revolt. About two
hundred Negroes of both sexes, all of whom had recently been
emancipated by the Proclamations of March, came one morning to
beg their former master, a certain Glenelg, to take them back into
bondage." I found myself getting interested, but closed the book
again.

I had an idea.

"Say—why don't we play at slaves?"

"How?"

"I whip you."

No reply.

"Come on," I said roughly. "Get your clothes off and lie face down on the bed."

I pulled out the belt of my trousers and held it ready. I'd never used a whip on a woman before. The novelty excited me. Natsue was taking her clothes off with a scared expression. There was something stylized about the way her hands and body moved. Memory stirred in me, reminding me of her connection with all those other men. Her body was slender but supple and in no sense thin. There was a kind of toughness about it that suggested that any marks from the belt would soon disappear. Her buttocks as she lay there on her face looked disproportionately large. With a quickening of the pulse, I felt the urge to beat her body till the black blood came gushing out. . . .

Without holding back, I brought the belt down on her buttocks. There was a smart crack, and I heard a groan deep down in Natsue's throat. A diagonal red weal started into sight on her flesh.

I won't deny that that first blow excited me. But simultaneously with it came a feeling that the ceremony was over. The next blow was fifty per cent habit, but this time a cry escaped Natsue's lips. It encouraged me to continue the beating. Lurching violently at each blow, her body gradually shifted toward the edge of the bed with a creaking of springs, till finally her lower half fell down into the gap between the bed and the wall.

"Stop, please!" she said in a faint voice, leaning over the bed with her breasts pressed against it, like a drowning man clinging to a piece of flotsam.

The face she turned to me as I stood on the bed was wet with tears. The expression and the tears had a kind of theatrical air. "So this is 'playing at slaves,' " I thought to myself. " 'Learning to relish my tears,' eh? But I can't see myself relishing *these* tears." And I let go of the belt.

"You mustn't stop," said Natsue at this point. "You're supposed to go on beating me, heedless."

"Supposed to as far as *you're* concerned," I said in a flat voice. "Oh, I know that all right."

The next moment, a surge of anger hit me. Suddenly I saw her as a lump of evil flesh. Grabbing her arm, I dragged her up and planted her firmly on the bed on her back. After I'd finished with her, I picked up the belt again and took a firm grip on it. As my eyes took in the thin, tender expanse of skin on her belly, her hands came up to cover it.

"Don't!" Her voice had a note of genuine fear.

" 'Don't' means 'go ahead,' doesn't it?"

"No, I'm scared. You wouldn't with an animal, even, if it was on its back with its stomach exposed . . . so defenseless and . . ."

The only kind of animal this suggested was not some creature of feline nobility and grace, but a rabbit. A rabbit with a pink, faintly shiny belly like a thin rubber membrane.

"Are you really scared?"

"Of course—I've never let anyone beat me before."

This excited me a lot. I flicked the belt lightly across her breasts, then, as her hands shifted leaving her belly exposed, brought it down with all my strength again.

That done, however, I realized I'd lost almost all interest; for me, it seemed, it was only a kind of ritual after all.

Natsue lay on her face making small sobbing sounds. The red weals stood out on the small of her back and buttocks.

"Does it hurt?"

"What do you think?"

"But it was good too, wasn't it? Women are all masochists at heart."

"It was nice for you too, wasn't it?"

"Just the once. I wouldn't want to do it again. I don't seem to have it in me."

"I wonder."

"Well, I don't. Strikes me I'm the sucker here."

At that time, I could still use the words lightly.

41

When I met Natsue five days later there were in fact no marks of the belt left anywhere on her body. I searched carefully, but couldn't even find any discoloration.

"I'm made like that," she said with a touch of boastfulness and the dewy look already coming into her eyes.

"My ears are sensitive," she added gratuitously.

I nibbled lightly at the lobes.

"Say something in my ear."

She had her arms raised above her head to expose the armpits, and her body was writhing slowly. I was struck as I watched by her skill in drawing me on. I breathed an obscenity into her ear. A moan escaped her lips, and her body reacted strongly.

It was all right that day. But the next time, when she whispered "Say something!" I felt objection and boredom at the idea of repeating the same thing.

"Just blow on it, then. That's enough."

"What d'you take me for?"

"My ears are rather special," she said in a more practical voice, though some of the wheedling overtone still remained. "I put perfume on my ears, don't I? Well, even the alcohol in it's enough to set them tingling as it evaporates."

"You've got some strange habits."

"It's not a habit—I was born like that."

She did, in fact, have a number of physical habits she'd picked up in her relationships with other men. Those lovers were always there, like a thin membrane between her body and mine. But in a sense it was this that allowed our affair to continue.

She had an attractive body. I liked her expression, too, when she was flushed with excitement; there are some beautiful women whom lust disfigures. I liked, too, the snug way she fitted in with my body. Physically, then, we were linked; but her body alone wasn't enough to tie me to her.

From around that time, the membrane between our bodies began to fulfill all kinds of functions.

"A man once died for my sake," she said.

I didn't like her when she said things like that. It smacked too much of narcissism. I shifted my angle to take a look at her. She thought she had men on a string, but it was really the other way round. I felt sorry for her. But what she'd said still bothered me.

"How did he die?"

"TB. He didn't want to leave me, so he refused to go to the hospital."

"And of course, being close to you meant . . . He was in love with you, wasn't he?"

"Yes, he was."

"I wonder, now." I laughed. " 'Every woman has a part that no man can refuse,' " I quoted. " 'Even the Buddha himself would get a little involved.' "

"I've heard that somewhere before."

"It's from Saikaku's *Five Women Who Loved Love*. You seem to have unexpectedly literary tastes. Anyway, I'm fed up with tales of true love. Let's have something a bit different. Something . . . shocking."

(Nearly a year later, Natsue was to say to me,

"I talked far too much. About the men in my past."

"You enjoyed it, didn't you?"

"It was *you* who enjoyed listening. That's why I talked, actually."

"I'm sure there's still some left to tell," I said. "Let's hear some more."

But in fact I didn't feel the same any more about that kind of talk. And her answer was,

"I've forgotten everything. Really. There's nothing left.")

"Shocking?"

"You've got a disgraceful past, so you must have a lot of shocking things to tell."

"Disgraceful? You pig!"

I could feel her breath coming faster even as she spoke.

Whenever I asked her about the other men she'd had, she would answer immediately. In time, she began to tell me about them of her own accord, and made herself excited in the process. In such ways, I got to know all kinds of things about Natsue and her lovers.

"Have you ever been raped?" I asked. She didn't answer at once.

"You have, haven't you?" I pressed.

"Yes. I hung onto the frame of the car window, but he dragged me into the hotel by force."

"Car? A cab?"

"He was driving his own."

"If you let a man like that give you a lift, part of you must have been willing."

"No! I never dreamed that kind of thing would happen. I went on struggling even after we got to the room, but he was awfully strong."

"So you said no at first."

"I *kept* saying 'no, no!' "

"Which changed before long to 'yes, yes!' I suppose?"

"That's right—'yes, yes!' with my tail waggling like hell."

She would deliberately say this sort of thing as we made love. The words would turn to moans, and she would arch her back, and move her body about. . . .

These conversations added a not unwelcome touch of spice to our relationship. As for the men, I asked for no details, and their faces and bodies remained decently obscure.

On another day, we had the following conversation:

"How many men do you know at the moment?"

"Why ask? Only you, of course, silly!"

"What's so silly about it? There were several before you moved, weren't there?"

"Mm . . . men I couldn't get rid of. But I broke with them just as soon as I could. Surely you remember? Though *you* only phoned me when you'd got nothing better to do."

I realized that after seeing Natsue, I'd never once fixed a time for our next date.

"But I never let you down, did I?" she went on. "Except in special cases. . . ."

I remembered calling when she had another man at her place.

"There must have been times when you arrived home after sleeping around and found him waiting for you?"

"There were."

"He must have sensed something and got suspicious."

"Yes, he did. I worked things so that we made love immediately, in case he checked up on me. Once he'd finished, I felt safe, because the white stuff was all mixed up inside me and he couldn't tell any more."

"You're a shocker!"

"But you *ordered* me to say something shocking, didn't you?"

42

One day, not long after I suggested "playing at slaves," Natsue said,

"Let's play at 'O.' "

No harm in letting her play the part just once, I thought. Everything was a thrill the first time, though from the second time on it always seemed to me like kid's play, and it never became part of our permanent repertory. For the moment, though, I couldn't think what I was supposed to do in practice. I'd read the book, but entirely forgotten the details.

"Brand me!"

"Brand?"

"To show you're my owner."

A vague memory of the end of *The Story of O* came back to me. A red-hot iron engraved with the "owner's" intials was stamped on the heroine's buttocks. When the wound healed, the shape of the initials was clearly discernible to the touch.

I remembered seeming to smell the scorched flesh as I read.

There were five strips of black velvet, about an inch wide, in a drawer of the dressing table. Natsue was naked. She held out her wrists and said,

"Bind them round me."

I chose two of the shorter strips and bound them round her wrists. They were fitted with hooks and eyes. Her hands were small, with slender fingers that hardly seemed to have joints. The effect was like handcuffs, though there was no chain linking the two black bands.

"My neck too."

A rather broader band, with three hooks sewn on ready.

"You made these yourself."

"Of course."

"Work for idle hands."

Even so, it excited me; it reminded me of a dog's collar. She lay on the bed face up, stretched out her legs, and said,

"My legs too."

It wasn't like being ordered about, or being a servant. There was a feeling that she was somehow ensnaring me, but I didn't have any urge to escape.

I bent over Natsue's legs and put the velvet round her ankles. As I did up the hooks, I grasped her ankle through the cloth and felt a slight stirring of emotion. Women who are very responsive sexually are supposed to have trim ankles. The ankle was slender enough for me to get my hand round, but it was a shade thicker than the other parts of her body would have led one to expect. Not that I'd thought about it in advance. The slight feeling of surprise as I grasped the ankle conveyed itself to her through my fingertips.

"You were thinking it was rather thick, weren't you?" she said with a chuckle.

I laughed without replying.

"But is it really, though?" she said.

"Just a bit. On you, that is. Why, was it bothering you?"

I stood up, and looked down at her naked body. Five glossy black bands of velvet were bound round in five places—her neck, her wrists, her ankles.

"Not specially," she said, looking up at me with dewy eyes. "I just happened to sense what you felt. Actually, people always said I had good legs, and so far I've believed them."

"You mean, a lot of *men* have praised them." A sudden suspicion arose. "Have you done this before?"

"What?"

"With the velvet."

"This is the first time. It's *your* brand!"

Her body looked sexy with the black "brands" on it. But in the end I only made love to her twice with them on. Not that I didn't believe what she said. I just got tired of it after the second time.

However, I didn't forget her saying, "This is the first time."

During the year following her move, I was so debilitated physically and mentally that I hadn't enough energy to strike up with any new women. I didn't even go with any call girls. Takako, Maki, and Yumiko had all gone far away, so I was left alone with Natsue.

I phoned her, and we met, at my own convenience. The calls were solely to arrange a meeting, and we cut out all unnecessary talk. As far as I was concerned, she was a body and nothing more. Even so, this kind of thing went on for a full year.

I won't deny that the men in Natsue's past—who were still there, a membrane between us—served as a welcome stimulant. And the desire to find some part of Natsue's body still free of this film that seemed to cover it so completely was another factor that kept our relationship going.

I tried hard to find something in physical relations with Natsue that would be a "first" for her—though having no taste for the so-called perversions, I left *that* field untouched.

More than once she said, "This is the first time." If she was to be believed, there were a surprising number of places on her body left untried.

The area behind her knees when she drew them up would get wet with sweat. It had always been like that, and I assumed it had been the same with the men before me.

But when I took her hand and put it against the place, she said, "That's the first time, too."

"You shouldn't tell lies."

"It's not a lie. I'm sure it's always the same, but nobody else ever pointed it out."

I'd already drawn attention to the sweat in the hollows there any number of times, but she'd never said anything like this before. This was nearly a year after she'd moved to her present apartment.

43

It was around the same time that a long-distance call came from my uncle.

"How're you feeling?"

"Rather better, thanks."

"Don't like to ask, but could you come down here at the end of the month? The boy's getting married, so we've got to have some kind of wedding. Only three are attending from our side—your aunt, you, and me."

I went, to the same small country town as before. As soon as I was alone with my uncle and his son, I said to the boy,

"Look, don't expect me to give a speech at the reception."

"Actually," he replied, "I've already given careful instructions about that to a friend of mine who'll be master of ceremonies." He gave me a knowing look. "No point in letting anybody get things off to an inauspicious start, is there?" It seemed that the idea of my presence had worried him, and he'd taken steps to prevent misfortune.

"Listen," my uncle said to him, dropping his voice, "don't you go getting the idea that a man really *needs* a wife."

Something in his tone of voice made this sound less like a warning than a sober reflection on his own past. I laughed in spite of myself.

"I must say, the trouble with you seems to have been women rather than wives," I put in. "All the same, I guess you get a lot of gossip in a small town like this. It must have taken a lot of guts to go ahead regardless. I admire you for it."

I really meant it—after all, in the big city you often don't know your neighbor's job, or even his name—but this time it was my uncle who laughed.

"Come off it! It's tough, I can tell you!"

"Really? Tough? But you still haven't learned your lesson?"

"Have *you*? Not that you seem to have got married after that once. . . ."

Had I learned my lesson, I wondered? I took a fresh look into my own mind. My ideas about women, it was true, had changed considerably since my youth. But no doubt that was due to forty-four years of life in which to observe women and have all kinds of dealings with them.

What about Keiko? Where she was concerned, I had quite a few painful memories, of which the business with Tsunoki was only one. They formed a cold lump lying at the bottom of my mind, visible if one peered in, but that was all. Since Maki left, I'd met Tsunoki once, and had heard nothing more from him. I didn't go to "Loco," so we never ran into each other there, either. The lump in my mind obstinately refused to come to life.

That was what I told myself, at least; but perhaps the wound inflicted by that episode was still there, covered with a thick scab? Had my experience with Keiko given me a mistrust of other women? I couldn't help feeling it was more than that.

"Lesson or no lesson," my uncle was saying, "you soon find another woman, don't you? In other words, you never learn. My elder brother—that was your father—he was much the same." A reminiscent look passed over his face. "It's in the blood. In the Nakata blood."

He turned to his son.

"Marriage . . . well, seeing you're with a big firm, I suppose you have to. People get funny ideas if you're not married, and it interferes with the job. . . . But make sure you don't have any kids. We've had enough of them."

No reply.

"Not as long as I'm alive, anyway."

There was a kind of earnest gloom on his face as he spoke.

44

The bride was in traditional wedding kimono, with a wig in the elaborate old-fashioned style.

The chalky makeup covering her face made the whites of her eyes look faintly yellow. Even her teeth, which were a gleaming white when she wore ordinary makeup, looked yellowish and dingy.

The flesh of her earlobes had a plump, swollen look. In accordance with some tradition—or with some fancy of the beauty specialist—the lobes had been lightly touched with rouge. The effect somehow suggested a fertility rite.

The moment I noticed them, I took a look at my uncle's face. "This woman will bear lots of children," I was thinking. When all was said and done, sex for a woman meant reproduction; most women themselves actually wanted it that way. . . .

In his formal black kimono with the family crest, my uncle stood looking straight ahead, a solemn expression on his face.

45

I stayed in that small country town for a week. Not that I'd any business there: if anything, I suppose I wanted to loaf around for a while before getting down to work on my next book.

Every evening, I went to the same *sushi* restaurant for a drink, then turned in early and slept.

On my return to Tokyo, I went straight to Natsue's apartment. Before, there'd usually been a week's interval between our meetings. But ever since she'd changed, the intervals had been getting shorter.

"How was the wedding?" she asked.

"All right. . . . Tell me, how old did you say you were?"

"I was twenty-four when I first met you. Why?"

"Nothing in particular. . . . How many lovers d'you have at the moment?"

"Oh, come on! You've asked me that before. No one but you, of course."

"The same answer as before. But this time we haven't seen each other for a week. You must find it frustrating."

I'd never before bothered my head about what she did in the

intervals. In the past week, though, I'd called her twice from the country.

"Frustrating?"

"You know what I mean."

"If *that's* what you mean, the answer's no."

"You get relief by yourself?"

"No, I don't."

"Be honest, now. I don't believe a woman made like you could go without it completely."

"It's true."

"What's true? You *do*, though, don't you? You'll have to show me how you do it."

Natsue's face by now was showing signs of excitement.

"Show me!" I commanded.

The room was full of bright light.

"Turn the light down," she said.

"But you never used to care how light it was."

Grasping the wrist she stretched out toward the electric light cord dangling from the ceiling, I guided the hand slowly toward her lower abdomen. A deep flush spread rapidly over her chest, and the fingers of the hand uncurled.

Suddenly, I remembered something. A young man who read my stuff would occasionally write me flippant letters about various serious topics. According to him, he'd tried keeping his mind blank while he was masturbating one night, and had completely failed to reach a climax.

"What d'you think about at such times?" I asked, standing looking down at her.

"Nothing."

"Your mind's blank?

"Right."

Presumably it was possible for a woman.

"But sometimes you think about things?"

"Yes."

"With who?"

"You, of course."

"There's that 'of course' again."

Abruptly she jumped up and got off the bed. Opening the closet, she rummaged in a drawer and finally came back with some black cloth in her hand. She'd kept the black velvet we'd used the year before.

"Here—since you can't check the inside of my head, you'd better put your 'brand' on me."

With unenthusiastic hands I wound the black cloth round wrists and neck and fastened the hooks. The cloth clung tightly to the skin there; but when I put the bands round her ankles they were quite loose.

Without noticing, Natsue pressed her right hand down between her legs, this time without any prompting.

Before long, her knees were drawn up, her thighs spread wide apart.

"Look," she cried in a thin voice.

Under the bright light, the small, crimson patch on the perineum strained as though being drawn deep down inside her. Several violent spasms changed to a weaker undulation, then to a slight flutter that went on for some time.

I remembered what I'd said about the vagina at the discussion with other writers more than a year previously. For me, I'd said, there was something evil about it. I'd be overjoyed if I ever managed to see it as a rose. . . .

The first time in my life that I saw one—a prostitute's—the leaden-colored lips were not swollen and curled back, but flat and shut like the slats of a persian blind, so that the pink interior (which I knew in theory I was to expect) was completely invisible. The effect was ugly. The result of this first experience was to put me off the sight altogether. Even so, I was fated to see it any number of times in the years that followed.

I'd been carried away by the discussion: "evil" was overdoing it a bit. All the same, the underlying nuance of the two words "ugly" and "evil" was different. One couldn't put it all down to that leaden color. I saw one once, in fact, that was like a moth with outspread wings—open and swollen, with the bright pink visible inside. The woman was young and behaved as though she'd already had experience with men. But as soon as she was beneath me she went suddenly still, and a faint frown of pain appeared between her eyebrows. She bled just a little. As soon as she had her clothes back on, she became the "experienced" woman again. After a few meetings, the pink edge began to take on a slightly darker shade. Being on the verge of middle age at the time, I found her pitiful and somehow touching. Despite this, my image of the organ itself was steadily transformed from ugliness to evil. . . .

Natsue was lying on her belly, her face buried in a large pillow. As I laid a hand on her shoulder blade, she shrank away.

"I'm embarrassed," she said in a small voice, her body wriggling. The smooth skin, faintly damp with sweat, moved beneath my palm.

My feelings at the moment were ambiguous.

At the point when she'd cried "Look," I'd thought her highly sexed for a woman, but not abnormal. Squeezing pleasure out of shame is a peculiarly feminine process. With men, I suppose, it's the exception rather than the rule; I, at least, have no such impulse.

Her pose, with her thighs spread wide apart, didn't inspire any disgust. But there was no flower, either.

I ran my hand slowly down her back. It was then that I noticed.

The buttocks, ample out of proportion to her slender body, were noticeably smaller than before. It wasn't that she'd lost weight, for the thin skin fitted the swelling flesh as tightly as ever.

I wondered if it was because of the "black blood" she'd lost, but said nothing. Tightening my grip on her shoulder and hip, I turned her over, then inserted a finger in the slack of the black band round her ankle and showed her.

"Well!" she exclaimed.

"Hadn't you noticed?"

"I wonder why?"

"I'm not sure."

"Do you think the velvet's stretched?"

"No, it's not that. Your neck and wrists are the same as before. Anyway, your ankles have got slimmer—you should be glad."

As I spoke, I felt a surge of violent excitement and, simultaneously, tenderness.

That same day I noticed another change in Natsue—though it, too, had probably been taking place gradually over a long period. Her voice, once low and rather husky, had become thin and clear.

"Your voice has changed."

"Really? I can't tell, myself."

"It's different at ordinary times, too."

Formerly the voice had been deep, with a kind of break in it. I'd seen it as a sort of self-defense or affectation, a possibly unconscious urge to present herself as a woman for whom life had nothing new to offer. By now, though, our relationship had reached a point where poses weren't necessary. She was relaxed with me, I thought.

"Even at ordinary times? I wonder why?"

"You're relaxed with me," I said simply.

"Oh dear! I try not to be, you know. I think it's important to keep a barrier between us."

It was just around then that I was feeling my own barriers going down. Her remark pleased me.

"I see," I said. "Let's say you're getting house-trained, then."

"House-trained, indeed! You make me sound like a dog."

"Why, don't you like being a dog?"

"I don't mind, but a dog has to be fed all the time."

"You mean it takes food from other hands too?"

I was on top of her during this conversation. After I spoke, I made a determined assault on her body. The thin, purified voice escaped her lips.

"That's it—that's the voice."

She said nothing. Tears welled into the corners of her eyes, where they grew into balls of liquid.

"Your voice had got heavy. It was choked with the white stuff from all those men you had to do with. Now it's gone, and your voice has improved."

"Ugh!"

The voice was vibrant with sensuality. The transparent balls at the corners of her eyes collapsed and ran down toward her ears.

"You've taken food from other hands since you moved here, haven't you?" I said, lightly slapping her wet cheek.

I'd spoken half jokingly, but Natsue's expression changed subtly, giving her face a childlike look. I felt a stir of surprise.

"No, I haven't," she said.

"Come on now, it's all right—tell me," I said, continuing to pat at her cheek. She swallowed, and her lips parted slightly. Then she shut them again and shook her head.

"I haven't."

Beneath the flush on her face there was a smooth pallor. Noticing it with a slight shock, I felt sure this time. "Well!" I thought to myself, with a mixture of surprise and sorrow.

"I know, I know, it's all right," I said. "How many times?"

She hesitated.

"Twice."

"The same man?"

No reply.

"I see: two of them."

Twice: that meant once with each. I felt doubtful whether it had really stopped at that, but I didn't press the point. Somehow the mental picture of myself slapping at her cheek to elicit a reply made me feel vulgar.

I could tell I was disturbed. When I first gòt to know her, it had been reasonable to suppose she was associating with a number of other men at the same time. But I was startled to find that she could have relations with other men even after she'd been almost beaten to death. During that period of nearly a year, she'd meant little to me except at the times I was with her, and I could understand if my attitude had driven her into other men's arms. But still. . . . I wondered whether Natsue happened to be made differently, or whether all women were the same.

I began to have a depressing feeling that I'd been childish to consciously risk visiting Natsue at her apartment simply in order to do the "manly" thing.

For the moment, though, there was no need to wonder whether Natsue was a special case or just an exaggeration of the typical. The immediate question involved one woman, Natsue, and one man, myself.

I took another look at myself.

I took a look at the woman Natsue, too.

I was pretty sure I wasn't saint enough to scoop her up in my arms—with all that was sticky, smelly, and obscene in her—and draw her to me.

Should I leave her, then? A year earlier, I'd probably have been only too glad to duck out that way.

But by now I needed her. It's her body you need, I tried telling myself. No strong resistance to the idea arose in me; but somehow I felt it didn't account for everything.

46

Around that time, a new and major change took place in Natsue's body. It showed itself in the feelings I had as I lay on top of her. It wasn't just something I happened to have overlooked so far: it was a sudden, definite change as though she'd acquired a completely different set of sexual organs.

Natsue had always functioned admirably in that respect. But now the functions began to intensify and diversify.

There was one thing in particular that was noticeable.

As the penis reaches the womb, then follows its outline in deeper until it's glued against it, it very occasionally happens that something like a fine, soft feeler stretches out and engages with it. The effect is of a lot of tiny bubbles fizzing against one's flesh.

I've met a few other women with whom this occurred, but even then it didn't happen often. With Takako it was like that two or three times a year. With Natsue, the effect was to come very frequently from now on.

In the middle years—sometimes even earlier—women tend to shut their eyes, while men open theirs. With time, the man's eyes open wider and wider; the stimulus of observing in detail the signs of pleasure in the body beneath his own helps prolong his own enjoyment. At least, that's how it was for a long time with me.

But the moment I felt that fizzing sensation, I instinctively shut my eyes and gave myself up to direct, undiluted pleasure unassociated with anything visual.

I became intoxicated with Natsue's body.

Day after day, I met her and took her to bed. I did so half unwillingly, since it meant I was getting steadily more entangled with one particular woman. But though conscious of the risks involved, I couldn't stop meeting her. It wasn't just the feel of her sex that attracted me; gradually, my whole body cleaved to hers. The same thing went on day after day, even while I wondered how soon I'd get tired of it.

Natsue had been fairly brazen right from the first. I sometimes wondered, even, if she got her kicks from deliberate exhibitionism.

159

What seemed still more likely, though, was that she'd had long training in tolerating bright electric light.

It wasn't till almost two years later that she'd started to complain of being embarrassed. The one thing she'd been shy about from the beginning was having people see her eat. Even after I dragged her along to the restaurant, she still disliked eating out.

"I'll get something at my place," she'd say. Even there, she'd sit next to me doing nothing while I ate.

"Why don't you have something too?"

"I don't . . ."

If I insisted, she'd shed all her clothes and tackle the food stark naked.

"I don't feel so embarrassed like this," she said.

That would excite me again, and I'd take her to bed. But my flesh was more than simply excited: part of it was being eaten away by her, too. Again I'd feel that same sense of dismay. But I still couldn't resist her body.

I wasn't young any more. Gradually, my body grew weary.

47

I was trying to get started on a new project. After seeing Natsue, I'd have a long sleep, then, refreshed, sit down at my desk. But for days on end the paper in front of me remained blank.

I had the strongest resistance to putting pen to paper. I'd make up my mind to start writing, but my pen came to a halt almost at once, and tearing up the paper I'd throw it in the wastepaper basket.

I resolved to plunge ahead and write a few pages regardless. I also decided I'd use a pencil with a soft lead for the purpose. An imported pencil. I've nothing against domestically produced goods, but in some fields they're definitely inferior. It always strikes me as odd, for example, how a Japanese-made red ballpoint pen always gets ink stains all over your fingers.

I set off for the local department store to buy myself a German 4B. I hadn't set foot in a large store for ages. I asked a receptionist for the stationery corner, then took the escalator to the fourth floor, where the girl had directed me.

I was walking along looking for the counter when I nearly collided with a child standing in the aisle. A small girl who reached to somewhere around my waist, she stood perfectly still, slowly tilting her head to the right. As she did so, her left arm, sharply bent at the elbow, gradually rose till the open palm reached the top of her chin, where it stopped. The five fingers, spread wide apart, stayed quite still.

Something about her movements wasn't like a living human being. I stopped and stared, wondering for a moment if a mechanical doll had invaded the aisle.

Then I realized that I was by the children's clothing counter, and that a mannequin dressed in the latest children's fashion was standing nearby. Its head and arm, mechanically operated, were slowly moving, and the little girl was moving her own head and arm in imitation.

What I felt at that moment was one of three emotions:

"That's a lovable little girl."

"Charming!"

"Now, that's interesting."

But which? Probably a mixture of all three.

Unconsciously my hand went out to pat the little girl's fringed head, then stopped in midair. Stepping around the girl, I went on, then halted and looked back. She was still repeating the same movements as the mechanical figure, an intent expression on her face.

If they were all like that—I found myself thinking—I wouldn't mind. The mixture of three emotions still persisted. No doubt about it, the feeling that she was a lovable little thing was one part of it;

but though I searched carefully, I couldn't find any real desire for children of my own.

Without warning, I had a mental picture, rather like an abstract painting, of my own semen discharging in the direction of Natsue's womb. Quite obviously, the action was sex disassociated from reproduction. A feeling slowly passed through my body that this act I so furiously engaged in, far from being linked to new life, was driving me ever closer to death.

The stationery counter was in one corner of the fourth floor. As I stopped in front of the case with rows of yellow and green pencils, I felt a dull, dragging fatigue around the ankles. I tapped at the floor with the soles of my shoes, and at the same moment pain gouged at a point somewhere in the muscles of my back. The pain passed rapidly, leaving a sense of foreboding in its place.

A few days earlier, an acquaintance had died suddenly of a heart attack, at an age that nowadays would justify the word "prematurely." An outstanding scholar in some scientific field or other, he'd also been notoriously fond of the bottle. In the end it had taken his life.

His wife told me at the wake that he'd been drinking only the night before. He complained of backache the afternoon of the same day.

He'd had a sharp pain, "like a gimlet," on both sides of the lumbar region. It hadn't stopped him from demanding beer, which he'd tried to open himself. But the hand holding the bottle opener wouldn't work.

A doctor was called. The doctor failed to make the association between back pain and the heart, and a few hours later my friend suffered a sudden heart attack. A year previously, another friend had died in similar circumstances. At that time there'd been a couple of doctors in attendance, but neither had succeeded in putting two and two together.

I recalled the smooth expanse of Natsue's belly and had a vision of my own body stilled forever on top of it. Was this the woman I'd selected as being *safe*? . . .

Nevertheless, once I'd bought my dozen pencils, it was to Natsue's apartment that my footsteps led me.

I could hear her voice saying inside my head, "A dog has to be fed all the time."

48

"Are you getting properly fed?" I asked Natsue.

"Fed?" she looked doubtful for a moment, then understanding dawned.

"Come on! You know perfectly well . . ."

"So you say, but—"

"Still suspicious? Just because you forced me to say I'd been fed by other men? I should have kept quiet. I really didn't think you were the kind to go on fretting."

True enough, at one time the idea of other men sharing her body hadn't bothered me in the slightest.

The one thing you need is Natsue's body, I reassured myself. *And you've got it here, now.* I felt the tiredness ebbing from my own body at the thought. Seeing me silent, Natsue went on,

"It was about three months after I moved here. There's been nothing since then."

"I couldn't care less either way."

"But it's *you* who's making the fuss."

The fact that she'd slept with other men since coming to this apartment concerned me only—I told myself—because of its bearing on women as a whole. I checked my own mind, even so, to make sure I wasn't just saying this to cover up some new possessiveness on my part. We were silent for a while.

"I've decided to be your slave," she said suddenly. "I've never felt that way before, but . . ."

I heard this with mixed feelings. Though Natsue's body had been cultivated by many men, and some of the seeds they'd sown had germinated, it was I, after all, who'd put the finishing touches. So I must have some reality for her, in terms of her own body at least. . . .

"Slave. . . ." I muttered to myself, picking up a book that stood next to a collection of reproductions.

"I've been looking at the preface to *The Story of O* that you're so keen on," I went on, opening the book and singling out a passage. "It says here, 'Yet there is nothing I can do to prevent this happiness from turning against you. The stone only sings more loudly when the blood flows freely and the body is at rest. . . .' 'Stone singing'—I wonder if that's from the Bible or something?"

"I couldn't say."

" 'Stone'—d'you think it can refer to the womb?" I said, recalling Natsue's womb, which would never be pregnant again.

"I wonder. . . ."

"You'd better watch out, though. Look how it goes on: 'Keep me rather in this cage, and feed me sparingly, if you care.' You see—in this book you've taken such a fancy to it says that it's best not to feed the woman too much."

"You know perfectly well what I meant by 'food,' " she said, looking into my face.

"Yes, and it seems a whip will do just as well. Or better still, a cat-o'-nine-tails."

"Don't be horrid! Even so . . . I do think she puts it well, don't you?"

"You mean you get pleasure from imagining yourself in the situations she describes?"

"Mm . . . I suppose so, in a way."

"You see—a whip *would* do just as well."

For the first time in some while, I pulled out my belt and took a firm grip on it. I brought it down mercilessly on her body, and went on doing so again and again.

A convincing groan escaped her lips. At the same time, her face took on a pitiful expression. This face of hers was another thing that had only shown itself recently.

The pitiful expression stayed a while, unexpectedly gave way to the look of a mature woman in ecstasy, then contorted violently as she reached a climax. Several times the same sequence passed across her face.

"Yes, she's satisfied with the whip," I thought.

If beating her was going to be enough, it would save me a lot of physical fatigue. But I got bored as the beating progressed, and began to feel foolish. I threw the belt aside, and plunged directly into the fray.

"I'm the sucker here," I thought to myself. I'd used the word lightly in a similar situation before, but now it carried a new weight.

But that thought too was swept aside in its turn. A bundle of extremely fine, subtly intertwined threads attached themselves to my skin and began to exert pressure on it. Sometimes, quite suddenly, they changed into a single thick thread and came forcing their way into my senses.

"Do I see you tomorrow?" I asked as I was dressing.

"I leave it to you."

"Hm."

"Just please yourself. Whoever heard of a master consulting his slave? If you hesitate, I'll sense it and start behaving like an independent human being."

"Maybe. But you've got a lot to say for yourself, considering you're a slave."

"No I haven't. I just want you to do what *you* want. If you don't need me any more, you've only to say so and I'll disappear at once."

The words could have concealed something sinister. They could even have suggested boundless self-confidence. But to me, knowing

165

Natsue as well as I did, they conveyed self-defense rather than self-confidence. They'd been thrown out to form a hard shell into which she could crawl and sit unseeing and unhearing. She was so sensitive that she behaved like this to avoid getting more badly hurt.

Some people might have found her attitude self-preoccupied, but I found it pathetic. I quizzed myself about this reaction:

"If you get too soft, you'll end up being torn to shreds."

"No—at the moment, Natsue's expressing what she really feels. But it's entirely possible that unless you keep reassuring her physically her words might turn into something different."

I could use the whip. Or there were various other indirect ways of satisfying her while she lay passive.

But I knew already that such things for me had become a kind of ritual that wouldn't stand up to repetition.

49

Summer ended and the signs of autumn grew more marked. A month had passed since I'd started meeting Natsue almost every day.

Even as things were now, it never occurred to me to live with her, and I always came home late at night. Getting into bed, I'd fall asleep at once. Sometimes, I had the feeling I might not wake up the next day.

One night as I came in through the gate, the sole of my shoe landed on a small stone, and I tipped sideways. I feel sure, at least, it was the stone that did it. My hand shot out and grabbed at a nearby tree to support me. The branches shook, and a shower of fine particles rained down on my head. The same moment, my body was wrapped in a gentle perfume; the tree whose trunk had saved me was a fragrant olive.

There are many different kinds of fragrance. Some stab at the nostrils, others seem gently to caress the membranes. Some are shallow, others have depth. Some force themselves insistently on you, others glance lightly away. For me at least, the scent of the fragrant olive is mild and soothing, with a strange power to transport me away from the present and into the distant past. The actual scene about me recedes steadily into the background—though without any sense of speed or hurry, despite the great stretches of time and space that are traversed in a brief moment.

Even after I'd gone indoors, the scent still clung about me. With one hand I brushed off the golden particles, each consisting of four petals, that rested on my shoulders.

I lay on the bed, and suddenly felt myself being drawn back—almost as though I were watching a slow motion picture, though it was all over in the space of one breath—to the point at which the forty-four years of my life had begun.

An odd sensation overtook me: strangely unbalanced, intellectually affronting. Deep down inside, my ears were blocked by a thick membrane which began to quiver delicately.

I turned over onto my face and put out one arm, letting it dangle over the edge of the bed toward the floor. My heart felt as though a massive hand might crush it at any moment. The feeling persisted, loaded with apprehension. My pulse was normal, no beats were being missed, yet the heart's regular rhythm began to seem like the second hand on a clock marking off the moments before the time bomb bursts.

"You mustn't move," I told myself. I lay perfectly still there on my belly, resisting a violent urge to get my body up and away.

If I tried nowadays to remember what happened during my period of deep depression, I seemed to have forgotten many things, or to have lost my sense of the order in which they occurred. Probably it was because I'd been so utterly washed out at the time. Another thing I noticed was that, during that year, my powers of self-observation were dulled too.

Now, unexpectedly, I recalled a scene that took place one winter's day. I'd been having spasmodic fits of burning my clothes and papers, or of making up bundles of my books and selling them off. I'd dug a pit in a corner of the garden specially for the purpose. It was raining, and I knew the fire was liable to go out. All the same, something drove me to get out of bed, slip sandals on my bare feet, and go out into the garden with an umbrella in my hand. I began burning notebooks from my apprentice days as a writer, along with old cotton kimonos and underwear. I used the umbrella more to shelter the pit than myself, but still the fire kept dying down, so I brought a dead branch I found lying on the ground and used it to stir up the flames. My one idea at the time was to reduce the things in the pit to ashes just as soon as possible.

The umbrella I'd used was a pale mauve, oiled-paper umbrella that Yumiko had left behind (though I still wonder why she'd possessed such a thing). I could vividly recall the faint smell of oil, and the mauve that must have tinged my face the same color. The collar of a damp cotton kimono had caught on the end of the branch and dangled from it like a limp, flattened body.

At that period, I was on my way to becoming a has-been, at least as an author. The idea of living "just because there's nothing better to do," which I'd always believed was present somewhere in my mind, failed to mean much to me. It might have been because my situation was too desperate, or because I'd lost sight of my own identity. In theory, the idea could easily have tied up with a feeling that I was ready to die at any time, but as soon as I was able to appreciate the crisis I grew apprehensive.

I lay scarcely breathing, waiting for something to pass; eventually, sleep must have descended on me. . . .

A pale pink, shining membrane was stretched out in front of my eyes. As I watched, the area within its outline was gradually magnified till the expanse of wet color occupied my whole field of vision. I could see what seemed to be ridges running over its expanse. The difference in height between ridges and depressions gradually increased till, all of a sudden, the low-lying parts were filled with a white, viscous fluid.

The pale pink of the wall before my eyes grew steadily darker. I could see the white liquid dripping stickily from it.

Then, reaching a shade close to crimson, the color unexpectedly began to fade, yielding in turn to the faintest of pinks. As it did so the white fluid, quite suddenly, disappeared.

I felt somewhat calmer.

Just then, filaments fine as silk thread began to grow out of the membrane at various points. Seven points in all, perhaps. Slowly, they grew longer. The feeling wasn't of fiber, though, but of something more metallic—copper wire, say.

The metal filaments stretched steadily farther out of the expanse of flesh. All seven of them had grown to a length of about four inches, and a strong sense of disgust was overtaking me again when, suddenly, a diamond-shaped piece of foil appeared resting horizontally on top of each thread. It was as though unseen hands with the thin flakes of metal held between their fingers had placed them, all together, on the tips of the feelers.

The underside of each diamond was a dull silver, but the surfaces were all of different colors. The one thing in common was that they were all pastel shades. Pale blue, pale yellow, pale green—the effect was of a bunch of flowers in bloom.

Little by little, the disgust seeped away, like water soaking into already saturated soil.

"Why—it's beautiful!" a voice boomed—and I woke up.

So it had been a dream. I was still on my face, but the uneasy feeling around my heart had gone. I stayed in the same position for a while, without moving.

"Flowers. . . ." I thought. "But it was as if they were made of aluminum."

It was already morning. Bright light fell in a thin, flat wedge through a gap in the curtains. Gazing at the light, I thought of

Natsue's room: a shadowy room with the heavy curtains drawn, even in daytime.

"What's going to happen, I wonder?"

Various fancies came into my head and vanished again. The one certain thing was that I was going to that dimly lit room again today.

As I plunged into the entrance of the building where she lived, I caught a whiff of Natsue in the air. Nowadays, Natsue's body hadn't any real smell to speak of. Yet a faint odor hung about it, an odor that both stimulated the senses and induced a faint melancholy. I climbed the stairs and walked along the long concrete corridor. The smell grew steadily stronger: the smell that I was sure no one but I could detect. Soon it filled my nostrils, stiflingly oppressive.

I was standing in front of Natsue's apartment. I grasped the knob of the door. The dark room lay beyond.

Now available in Kodansha International's new paperback series:

Black Rain 黒い雨 by Masuji Ibuse
The Dark Room 暗室 by Junnosuke Yoshiyuki
The Lake みずうみ by Yasunari Kawabata
War Criminal 落日燃ゆ by Saburo Shiroyama
A Dark Night's Passing 暗夜行路 by Naoya Shiga
Botchan 坊っちゃん by Natsume Sōseki